Forbidden Tome

Forbidden Tome

Hansel and Gretel's True Tale

Jeffrey Underwood

iUniverse, Inc.
Bloomington

Forbidden Tome
Hansel and Gretel's True Tale

iUniverse books may be ordered through booksellers or by contacting:

iUniverse
1663 Liberty Drive
Bloomington, IN 47403
www.iuniverse.com
1-800-Authors (1-800-288-4677)

ISBN: 978-1-4620-6006-1 (sc)
ISBN: 978-1-4620-6007-8 (ebk)

Printed in the United States of America

iUniverse rev. date: 10/25/2011

Not for eighteen and under!

CONTENTS

ACKNOWLEDGEMENTS

Thank you to my muse and ever supportive wonder,

Penny Woodward

Thank you also to my character inspiration,

Rose Smith

Finally, thank you to two wonderful authors who provided

Me with erotic inspiration and the notion that

Altering perspective is a magnificent thing.

INTRODUCTION

This is a fantasy that turns the story of Hansel and Gretel upside down and sideways. The evil Stepmother in the original rendition is caring and supportive in this telling. The Witch has vanished to be replaced by a beautiful Vampire unique to the breed. It is a tale of lost children, conflicted and also devoted characters, blazingly intricate and heart felt adult erotica. Villains, heroes and heroines are all oh so human. Complexity rules this universe.

The setting is nineteenth-century Germany in the deeper forests, plateaus and rivers of that country. The children love their Father and Stepmother. It is Hansel and Gretel's desire to save their Stepmother that sends events spiraling out of control. Their parents plunge themselves into a desperate search to preserve the family integrity and return the young children back to the tender confines of their hearth and home.

Emotions are immediately intense. Juria and Claire have a dispute and suddenly find that their children have run into the forest in the middle of the night. Their pursuit of their children leads them into physical and emotional terrain that proves frustrating, mysterious, painful and sexually lush yet difficult as well.

Ultimately, their trek teaches them vividly of love, forgiveness and compassion. Yet the unexpected rears its head often.

Finally, with the aid of others, Juria and Claire discover the unknown kidnapper of Hansel and Gretel and struggle with what will become of their children.

It is a captivating story of emotional alterations, erotic heat, and a way to survive the inevitable challenges that they meet over and over in their adventure.

Chapter 1

Blood Curse

Viktoria knew her only neighbors in the surrounding forest were those dwelling in the house of the woodcutter. Long before Viktoria was transformed into the beautiful monstrosity that she was now, she had the faint ability to collect images of others' lives. A psychic ability, if you will. Now as the undead, that ability had been multiplied one hundred fold.

Her images of the woodcutter, his wife, their children, Hansel and Gretel, were definitely ones of sadness and discord.

The inky black heavy cloak of night clung tenaciously to the surrounds with the light of a full moon pounding down where it was allowed to go.

Viktoria was standing solemnly and in full concentration. This was when her uncontrolled blood lust commanded her. She was its slave.

Being a slave to anything offended her sensibilities, vampire in the flesh or no. Before her transformation, independence grounded her being as nothing else ever had! To submit to a stronger force than herself was nothing more than complete capitulation. She loathed being submissive ever, anywhere, anytime.

Once she had had a heart that shrank from isolation, expanded with love of others. She had loved being social, being charming, being genuine, empathetic and supportive.

Now she had fallen to the other side, the side of darkness, of impulse. Yet her heart beat still as it had in her past. It beat for the sake of beauty and goodness. The conflict now within that organ of hers was excruciating, painful and often devastating.

The hunger, the bloodlust both crept upon her in the most peculiar manner. Before she realized her hunger, her thirst, her pulse would quicken.

But the peculiarity was that it would only quicken thrice each time in a separate location: first, an insinuation of pulse in midnight nipples, clit in immediate thrall to the feeling then and finally, a hard pulse at her core.

There was never an alteration to this pattern of her hot nipples, her welling and reddened clit, then wetting sex. The urge to relieve the growing pulses there were utterly huge, entirely unstoppable.

So she lusted as humans' lust, experienced passion as she had pastime, desired a sweet and good connection with humans because, yes, she actually was sweet and good. But then she would drink as only a vampire can drink.

Standing there, still, senses on edge, her nipples full, her sex drenched, she was thinking of relief, of course.

She felt her heat as if she were a furnace. To delay satisfying that gorgeous throb was all that consciously gripped her mind. Because she knew that collapsing into that heady and overwhelming sensation was to explode in orgasm, lose any of her remaining humanity, and find droughts of rich red blood to drink, to drain and to transform her victim. This was to subdue her lust for a blissful moment until she hungered again.

She could reach for herself to provide orgasm.

By her eyes, her wondrous looks, her infinite strength, she could make others reach for her to provide her orgasm. Whether her victim kneeled before her and tasted her or entered her with their shaft flaring and thick in monumental heat, they were her victim. They would yield and submit. They would surrender their blood to her.

In the moment of plunging her teeth into an artery so abundant in ripe sustenance for her, she would hate herself. Hate her loss of control. Hate that her memory of herself before her metamorphosis was her heart's desire . . . that is to be a woman of kindness and compassion, a woman who desired to do no harm.

Or actually even enhance someone else's life.

Yes, she could transform others into what she was. This endless perdition, endless torment that stalked her without relenting. Some would say that would be a gift, the gift of life eternal. Ah though, that was to be deluded. Infinite torment was no gift!

Chapter 2

Reflection

The woodcutter's wife, his second, was gently looking into the mirror at herself. Making light assessment of what the subtleties of her loveliness consisted of. She was not vain. Simply bewildered and saddened at her present plight. She wanted to observe if this sticky weight of sadness could be seen by her here and now. Did it change her appearance? Was the bluish sense so ethereal in substance that it had no noticeable effect on the glow that she had been born with?

Ordinarily, she was vibrant, confident, assured . . . a mindset toward her life of positive outcome. Any other flow was strongly disconcerting to her. Yet here it was that rare, but enlarging sense of feeling amiss, something amiss. Was it herself? Her passionate but possibly flawed union with her husband? Could it be the children? No, never that, never the children. On that she was adamant!

Within herself, she felt the unraveling of good intentions upon her part. She had compromised with Juria. Was that unwise?

She had felt a very dynamic flaring desire upon first encountering him. She had been strolling on the forest verge in a moment of escape and solitude. He was there suddenly, yet far from her view but near enough for her to feel the flaring desire, that lightning strike to the heart, as she froze in place, only glancing at his form to begin. He was slashing rhythmically at an angle cut near base of massive fir tree. Over and over, his ax arched identically, chips flew freely. His shirtless shoulders tensed and relaxed. She was in pause only briefly. She could be exquisitely impulsive and was now. Forward she moved.

4

As a man of the woods, therefore of acutely tuned senses, Juria stopped and turned. He glanced down shyly. He was not accustomed to being approached shirtless and sweat soaked. She could tell that. And, as would be expected, they passed glances and then talked.

Claire remembered how drawn she was to Juria. His sensual shyness and robust physique compelled her. Put succinctly, his ass and hard plated muscles caused her sex to dampen. And this intensity of response had never riveted her being before Juria.

Even now, as she ruminated on that first encounter, her vault swelled and pulsed and became moist. She never doubted their desire for one another. It was almost a yearning, a constant thread of ache throughout the day long.

In their case, this passion created an enormous mutual emotional bond. She sensed always his total effort to please her, to make her happy. Because she knew this so completely, she wanted to give back to him. And give back she did!

And that was the rub, one of the prime aspects of disquiet for her now. As she faced the mirror, she faced herself. She had compromised for him. She moved from large community to country, into a cottage house after having lived on an expansive, beautiful, well-tended estate. She went from wealth and activity to much reduced luxury, as she also went from activity to isolation and solitude. Willingly, she made these sacrifices for him. She loved him. But she asked herself, in spite of that love for Juria, if she could forever hold to this compromise, this altered and reduced style for her.

Claire closed her eyes as if blind. She brought her fingertips to her broad and high set lovely cheekbones, to her full and warm lips, to her sweetly rounded chin, over the crested tip of nose, fingertips rustling her long and lush eyelashes, thence to long expanse of forehead. She pushed fingers through a field of fine, lengthy, auburn-blond tangles. Claire bent her neck back then. She opened her eyes as if startled by a loud sound. Yet it was not a sound of any kind. It was nothing, though, except the burst of sensuality she felt as she massed her hair backwards with her hands.

Claire knew her sensuality already though. She wanted to know whether sadness was visible upon her, possibly a subtle line that had not existed earlier. A tiny crease or two at lip corners from a frown worn steadily. Subtle, not subtle, anything!

Were there other than the uncertainty of her strength to maintain her compromise for Juria? How deep did love go? But yes, yes sadly, there were other impediments. That word 'sadly' for Claire cropped up over and over lately. Oozed from her mind, fell in whispered fashion from her lips, appeared an instant with each heartbeat. What else lurked that made her sadness even darker?

Easy that. It was Juria's first wife who lingered yet in his mind. She had been lithe and lovely, Danika. That name dwelt in Claire's questioning parts. Claire respected Juria's love for Danika as something frozen and in his past. Had he fully moved on though? A moving on that allowed him to give full attention to the present; a present of Hansel and Gretel, Juria and Danika's children together.

Claire, unconsciously, drew away from that sadness; those unsettled feelings roiling inside of her. She had to! Had to now! So she dropped both hands down to her nipples and began mindlessly stroking and pulling on those big brown and now stiffly urgent tips.

She heard a sound . . . real this time. She rapidly placed her hands onto her lap. Her hands became passive and still. It was Juria.

Chapter 3

His Domain

The tiny home stood solidly on verdant and lush ground; ground on forest margins with a canopied tunnel of hoary, thick bristling-branched trees ever present. There was no entrance there that was not dank and musty. Juria had dwelt in this place perpetually, never another place for him. He would have it no other way, would be nowhere else. He was fascinated by what others feared. And he knew the terrain so well. This was his comfort, his zone.

He was equally as certain that this was not Claire's comfort. She had made a compromise for his sake. He loved her. And wanted her to feel regard as he felt regard for the wood and its blessed tranquility. She would not yet. She was a much softer creature than he. Not just in gender or form but also as to her instincts. She craved much more than remoteness and separation from most all. He would do all that it would take though.

Her hesitation at accepting his abode did not stop his wild desire for her. Claire had saved him, was still saving him from the torment of his having been a widower.

Claire was nearly all that he had ever needed to be pitched into outer limits of ecstasy and sensuality. She was astoundingly gorgeous physically and spiritually. Her high energy ignited her abandon in bed. Her want that all be well left him breathless. Her grace and deep beauty compelled him forward, provoked a deep set yearning for her. It was a yearning without surcease. Claire had length of strands that shone and swirled so delicately as she moved her head. There was hint of underlying auburn tint to the woman's otherwise blond earthward fall of hair. This shimmer of silk surrounded a face so stunning that all beholders' eyes were magnetically drawn. Her skin radiated soft light and cream hues that dramatized wide green eyes and arched cheekbones. Eyelashes beckoned. Their length pleaded for gentle touches of lips to lashes, kisses mindless and sweet. Her lips were equally as compelling and often with a moist sheen holding sway at their surface.

From her face, looking down, one would then have seen the curving rounds that were soft, pendulous breasts. The simple press of those big breasts against clothing was delicious as it was now in this revelry of her. His mind skimmed quickly over the remainder of her body: the breathtaking contrast of petite figure with her dramatically large breasts, those sculpted round ass cheeks, those legs elegant and proportionally short, and such strength there as well.

His chest felt prickles of warmth. His nipples grew.

Without so much as a sound, he slipped through the door to the house and nearly floated across wood flooring to where he hoped that she would be. His timing seemed that of utter perfection as she was rapt at her mirror. Her gaze was so intense, she was motionless. She had removed all of her clothes for reasons he was unsure of but appreciated nonetheless. He felt his cock shift position as it enlarged. Blood flew into his organ as he continued to stare. He knew that he shouldn't secretively look but could not help himself. He leaned down to her and let his faint warm breath caress her neck as he whispered to her "stand up please my lovely Claire."

Her thrall with mirror was broken. She stood for him slowly. She was so tiny from behind. She moved almost as if she had been paralyzed and the effort to stand had cost her much. As she stood, she paused; brought her hands back to his temples and gently stroked his scalp and pulled him down to her. It was such a touching gesture but so brief too. Still whispering, he asked after the children. In bed, fast asleep was her answer. He gently traced a finger up the divide which separated her smooth buttocks. She shivered a moment at this. His cock was encased in his trousers. That unruly column of his pushed the canvas material of fall front to bigger bulge. The vivid stretch of trouser material displayed his silhouette perfectly. Claire pirouetted, facing him. Tiny encapsulated her description but for her lusty upper curves.

His passion for her rose . . . and rose some more. He gently stroked her pendulous creamy curves. With each stroke, she breathed more deeply, more quickly. That served to thrust her nipples into his torso. He gazed down at her curved mounds. Her faint bluish venous lines drew a map down to her aureoles; aureoles deep brown, large, compelling. And deep brown, very stiff nipples. Points of heat pressed into him.

Claire had tipped her head back slightly. Her soft, sensual flesh jutted into him even more because of her movement. He was being invited by her. He accepted that invitation with hot greed and so brushed his minutely open lips over her nape, over her throat, lingered at apex of breasts. He inclined his head forward at an even more severe angle. Bent some, knelt some. He knew that she felt his hands cup her breasts, that she felt his mouth intensively as he suckled her nipples, one, and then the other. Her heat transformed into flame. Her eyelids closed almost fully. He had looked up momentarily and could see that.

He held her midline above her hips and at her lower back with one arm. Claire surrendered into that arm of his He moved the chair with his other arm and guided her up onto the shelf forward of the mirror for her to sit again. He inclined her against the glass of the mirror. It was cold but she seemed not to notice at all. She was already swept up in their passion dance.

She fractionally spread her legs for him and moaned. He continued to gorge on her ever swelling nipples. The huge bounty of her breasts kept him passionately sucking those gorgeous nipples stronger and harder. Yet he also reached a hand of his down to spread her nether lips wide and used his middle finger to stroke her hot red knob there.

Claire pushed herself toward his hand and clenched and unclenched her thighs once, twice, moaned again. Her trembling began at the site where he touched her with his hand. Her hand reached for him. He threw his hand over the buttons of his work shirt and tore one half of the shirt away from his body. It hung there on his other arm, the arm with the fingers that played upon her clit. He gripped her reaching hand and placed it on his exposed nipple.

She stroked his nipple languidly. He was hard as he could ever be. The pulse in his organ was huge, made that much more by its captivity in his trousers.

She equally slowly placed her other hand over his hand that was on her sex. Her sex throbbed so exquisitely as she slightly pushed their hands more insistently over herself. Her flushed reddened knob gathered heat from that. She wanted him desperately. Yet something unsettled her.

As a female can, Claire sat up straight and opened her eyes wide. "No, I cannot my love. I have to know that you truly love me before any more of this."

Juria was almost in pain. The urge to pound into her was demanding, more demanding now that he had been refused when so close. But he respected and loved her so much that he complied.

Chapter 4

The Children

Hansel and Gretel were not asleep.

They had the only real luxury that the cottage offered, a small yet beautiful bedroom. Gretel's bed was closest to her parent's bedroom and Hansel's next to Gretel's. Hansel was in his usual deep slumber Gretel thought.

Gretel was not. Though faint, she could overhear Juria with Claire. Gretel was frightened because she had heard unusual rustlings between Juria and Claire. Not anything that she recognized. It was not that precisely which had caused her fearfulness. It was what transpired after. Claire had definitely spoken to Juria . . . about love. That's when Gretel's misgivings had begun. A pause between her parents occurred then.

Hearing Claire move rapidly and then listening to her definite smack of paper on hard surface shocked Gretel. It was, to Gretel, a warning sound, a high alert sound. She did not want it to be but all of her child's instincts told her that it was.

Then all became indistinct, if not almost silent. Time stretched and elongated for Gretel. She did not like it at all. Then when she heard the sound of her Stepmama's hard and swift pace to the cottage front door and her determined exit from the cottage itself, at night, was more than Gretel could bear. Maybe Hansel had even been woken by the fracture in the midnight calm. Gretel had to check with Hansel. Now!

Hansel was drowsing. The sleeping boy was restless. He was not able to find that completely satisfying position. Something was disturbing his deeper senses too that was making for a rash of unsettling dreams.

Small feet pattering briskly, yet carefully across the room to his bed surprised him into immediate and total alertness. Sister Gretel was now at his bedside, frowning, intent, eyes slightly damp at the corners. Hansel leaned in toward her anxious face and placed hands on her shoulders gently. "Gretel, little one, what, what is it?"

"Hansel, Papa and Stepmama, I think they are fighting. I don't know for sure. Did you hear anything, anything at all? I am scared, Hansel!"

Hansel shushed Gretel and simply stated, "Tell me quickly what you know."

Gretel replied, out of breath or as if, "Stepmama left the cottage just now. She went out the front door. Papa was so quiet as I heard nothing from him. He didn't stop her! She doesn't know her way. Should we follow and bring her back?"

Hansel was unsure momentarily of the woods at night. As a young male would, he stopped his thoughts abruptly. He and Gretel loved their warm and gentle Stepmama. She was not their mother but was so sweet and protective of them. As if they were her own. She and Juria had no children yet between the two of them. Hansel sensed that for Claire, he and Gretel were children of beauty and innocence. Children she loved as Juria's children but also simply because of their pureness and innocence. Gretel reminded Claire of herself at that age, Hansel suspected.

And Claire was always dumbfounded by how protective he was of his little sister. Not just protective, also treating her as his equal, almost. Hansel supposed Claire deemed that he was wise much beyond his years. And he knew that Gretel was finding her own wisdom through him as well. Hansel wished to make Claire's heart swell in pride and feeling for them.

That their Papa and this partner, their Stepmama, their Claire, had argued was unique. Actually, it terrified both children so badly because it had never happened before. And Claire's knowledge of the forest was much less than theirs. She had to be rescued!

Hansel tightened his fingers on Gretel and spoke urgently. "We will go out the window! Here's a fur to throw over you. I will do the same. We have to help get her back to the cottage. She could get lost!"

Hansel tore two furs off his bed and tossed one to Gretel. He kept the other for himself. Hansel had a dried piece of bread he had grown tired of from dinner last and had perched it on the windowsill. He grabbed it. Then, with his lead, they both easily squirted through their low open window. In their haste, bare feet, no caps, only furs seemed natural to them. They were kids, after all. Impulse had seized them. They only thought to save their Stepmama, their Claire.

Into the night they flung their energized bodies.

Hansel did not hear Juria calling to them. Juria had not heard their exit. Claire was elsewhere and otherwise occupied. Hansel prayed that they would find her rapidly.

The cold, dank mixture of prickling grass blades and the clutching suck of raw wet earth surrounded their every footstep. Each footfall was as stealthy as they could manage. Toes tingled at both the unexpected damp and the rush of adrenaline through all of their young limbs. Hansel went where he thought Claire would most likely have gone. Gretel was his contrail, his permanent contrail. She was desperate to keep up.

Hansel glanced forward and backward repeatedly. He did not want to make matters worse by having Gretel lose her way also. Yet Gretel's five year old capacity to follow was frustrating for Hansel. He was much faster than she and so worried that he was somewhat heedless. Yet, responsible and mature child that he was he always had their security in mind. But Gretel's pace was still driving him crazy. "Hurry, hurry, Gretel and move as fast as you can!"

Gretel was doing all that her tiny body would allow her. She cried, "Yes, Hansel. I am. I am. Please find her!"

Hansel was not noticing the thickening surround of timber creeping around him and his sister. His sister was totally focused on Hansel's movements and keeping up as best as she could. Dark became darker. Tree edge closed in upon them. Their tortured breathes as they pursued their Stepmama subtly grew.

Gretel had no surcease of fear either. They had seen nothing of Claire and were dropping further and further into the deep hole of the forest; a forest that they had felt confident that they knew well and that this confidence had served them well in the past. But it was pitch black now. They hadn't ever explored the tree studded expanse this way before. Hansel dropped the breadcrumbs therefore. He had felt clever but sadly, the breadcrumbs had run out long ago. At most, those breadcrumbs would feed the birds he imagined. They would no longer be helpful to Hansel or Gretel.

But the strain to find Claire was unstoppable for both. They wanted no harm to ever come to their Stepmama. As it had to their real Mama! There was no turning back. Ahead was their only course!

Chapter 5

Danika's Missive

Claire gazed at Juria with rapt and questioning eyes. She slid off the surface and walked deeper into their bedroom. From a drawer of hers, she removed sheets of paper. Air went out of him. He sat. Claire dropped it in front of him and said "You saved this. That is not my complaint. You hid it from me. That is my complaint. Why?"

Such a unique missive, that. One he cherished almost above all others from her . . . or anyone for that matter as a spontaneously written expression of love and dedication to Juria in his youth from Danika in her youth.

It was such an early awareness of Danika's innermost erotic responses. It meant so much to him . . . Danika's trust in Juria. That she could reveal such genuinely personal information to him! It showed such bravery and precociousness from her also. Parents deemed little girls to not know or reveal such shameful abominations as she revealed to Juria.

She, Danika, had been his sweet first love and was his once wife now dead.

He did not, could not, resist reading it again as it lay near him even as Claire dressed herself in obvious uncomfortable determination to be neither nude nor so exposed.

His eyes skimmed this:

"After you leave, I reluctantly close the creaking door on your receding back. Hansel and Gretel have left just before you with glee for school. Should I immediately dress and follow to catch you soon thereafter, even if unseemly bold for a woman to do? In that elongating pause of uncertainty, I notice the memorable aura our place of living makes me feel. Turning slowly, I look around for a casual caressing few minutes. My eyes drink it in as has been done so often before today. Our abode's shapes, temperatures, materials and textures cause my body to feel absolute freedom.

I do not return to bed. I feel, as I always do, the windows presence and the awareness of calm space; this for me is a tantalizing, knowing sensation.

The unexpected is my goal between you and me even if it sneaks past the ordinary behaviors of a wife for her husband. As long as it always shows you that I love you exquisitely, I am content.

Seed of plan, unusual plan for today, germinates. I can do no other than smile as I contemplate the details. I feel a strong urge, deeply flavored to satisfy one or the other hunger and begin the action of nibbling on a slice of freshly baked bread. Plain it is. I choose to savor the soft spongy texture and grainy yet light smell of it. It is nothing complex. I am surprised how frequently I feel this ease and naturalness in our abode. All that I can do in our home I do out of love, rarely necessity. And then I swallow my last bite of bread which I have mixed with several berries also.

I find our room, our bed and gently lie myself down on it. This is a luxury that I almost never indulge in. Yet I have to oblige it this morning. Forces inside of me will not yield and I must quench them. I will only take moments to accomplish that. Ha ha.

This desire in me is strong and of a unique form. I need to know and to experience the more rampant love making person who is me beginning with my own wants to be a penis. My mind believes that you most certainly have imagined what it must be like to have a vagina. Not just suck on one and be there but to feel a cock at your opening, against your inner walls? And not just in your mouth, although that is a great, desirous thing as well.

Please do not be shocked here. I trust you so well that I feel ready to empty the chalice of my honesty into your sweetly, gently cupped hands.

Looping back to my exposure, I feel like being a cock. And I do not even think of size. That has nothing to do with this moment of pleasure for me. I cannot expend the smallest of energy on that for the huge looming prospect of being a cock is all that I need to feel. I urgently want to seduce another part of myself. Ah yes, that part that is the limitless woman in me. Now, since I can remember times when I have sought my release myself, it is without difficulty that I initiate advances towards her in a fully pleasing manner. And all the while, I know and cherish that the woman who lies passive is me. I am very uninhibited. And this surrounds the excruciatingly sensual fact that I love to realize when you now come down on me and that is that you are totally without hesitation. It is an act that is so ungodly rare of men to do. Though not you! You are in fact breathlessly craving that particular contact with me. It makes it so exciting to know, thrilling to actually have, not simply a wish for the future, as it was for me once. And I now incorporate this entirely new and abandoned lust in my own manipulations of myself.

Many thoughts are going through my head as to how I have made myself reach a peak in my past. It has always been difficult as I knew of no other young girl who would ever do the same as me . . . or, Heaven forbid, tell anyone of it even if they did. And my parents . . . oh my god, their shame, if they knew, would be eternal! Some of these erotic actions were to be repeated sometimes, sometimes not; such as with the maid's old broom that was left to cast a shadow over the kitchen corner perpetually. To let it remain there, no, that was not to be because of me. Simply put, I found my chance to sweep it away and no one ever noticed its absence hence. I always used it to simply rub against its smooth and hard surface. I always secured it at an angle into a corner in my bedroom so that I could ... would you dare smile at this revelation? ... you had best not ... climb up the broom handle. This from climbing urges that have come with me wherever I have gone. And this physical building up of my body to the broom top applied the sweetest pressure imaginable at the time. Eleven was my age then. I was not even aware of the word precocious. I also did not know of any aspect of my loins either. Just that it caught and kept my attention. My own body weight applied exquisite pressure to my clit. I now know its naughty name. I just had to rub and excrete juices and go up and down slowly. My wetness made me feel very sinful and, conversely, free; so free for me to rub up and down, over and over. No matter the soreness after. And that always made it so hard to wait for it to become pain free. Then I would do it again. I had no urge to place anything into that unknown space. That then was even too much for me to imagine.

I became more creative with the slow passing of time. Here is what I mean by that. I wanted an outdoor experience but a discrete one, obviously. So I searched outdoors at length. Ah, but without success. One dinner, my father was mentioning some of the rare trees that he had found bordering our home. When he mentioned bamboos sheltered below a stand of canopied leafy trees. I was amazed. I thought of the privacy, their roundness, and the almost perfectly smooth surface and that they yield without breaking. A throb went through me. For years, I soaked those bamboo trees all along their green perfection in that invisible space. I remember one early summer afternoon in particular, my love. Instead of simply clinging to the bamboo while standing, I took what slight running leap that I could and climbed that tenderly strong and yielding tree to an off ground height that suited me well. Having reached the top good gripping portion of its sturdy trunk, I experienced a real desire to hang on and make gravity supply me with this crazy pressure, crazy feeling rising out of that hungry juncture of mine. This caused me to grit my teeth and try to climb all the way up it, dangling my legs, letting my bulk move of its own weight except to deviously insure that the focal point of bamboo pressure confined itself to my sensitive bud. I hung there for as long as I was capable. This hidden aspect, that I was not seen nor was my whereabouts known, was so delightful that I found myself often absent from home for short bursts of out of sight delight. I was so greatly surprised when I first softly moaned at the pressure of wood upon my hot tip there. Soon I lost the sense of my moaning in the rising heat of my excitement. I held my release as long as I could. It felt so good to build that expanding sensation of mine. But I also would feel the sad need to leave once having completed myself. So, instead of yielding to my heat quickly, I would almost get to that fantastic point, then slide on down, run back to the stands edge, my wetness unbelievable, and turn and almost lunge back toward the bamboos, my friends, and leap again at the strongest of them. I would hold on tight as that one would sway to and fro, caressing me as I craved. I would lean forward and be pressed against the hardness. Then the pressure would tease away as I leaned the opposite direction.

In the present, I use that approach in my caresses to myself or within our lovemaking . . . applying and then softening pressure so that my mind and body swirls in delirious pleasure as it used to those years ago.

And no wonder my attraction to someone who works with and around wood.

You are my lovely woodcutter, Juria."

Chapter 6

Danika's Missive Concluded

Juria could not tear his eyes away from the seductive pull of his lost love's letter. Even as Claire's footsteps leaving the cottage pounded on his eardrums, he could not put Danika's letter down. Here is more of what he could not resist:

"Then, I used to always tense up my legs because of the pressure. Well now, I prefer many times to feel like I am hanging free. So today, I use that feeling to really get me to lie freely wide open, legs wide as they can be. I am sure that it is a freedom of submission to you when I lie so completely open and available; so fully open that my juices flow and rise and flow some more.

Alone, that position impels me to a penetrating level that is extreme. In your presence, at your request, you must look at me and resist your impulse to touch, and then I shudder in delight and definite anticipation. The knowledge that you are watching all of these thousands of changes flow on in me is so sublime. I cannot tell you how delicious it is! My ache escalates severely then and even more when I ask you to barely touch me. The tease is so wildly stimulating for me.

So today, I make the woman in me wait. She lies there for an extended time with the man just peering. She wants to writhe but holding still, unmoving, built the passion into her like a deeply driven wedge. And it is so amazing that he knows exactly how to satisfy her. Slowly and lasciviously he toys with her, the male in me in control; that male having total knowledge of how to satisfy me. He is so male; perfectly so. With this patient male scrutinizing her, she grows drenched in need to be touched. And when it is quite time, he guides his fiery column to her thigh.

Her eyes are closed. She is physically warm as she simmers in her passion divinely. He lightly flicks the swollen bud there. That tiny throbbing knob of hers is so in thrall to him. The touch puts a real surge down her legs and mound to arch and meet this thing where it is above her. It comes down to meet her.

And I remember another place, same time, different area of the grounds. This was lovemaking to an iron bar bannister riding either side of ramrod straight downward pitched steps at a close at hand chapel for all neighboring folk to attend. The odd angle of this bannister helped me to control the touch advantageously. I recall learning to heave my body up to meet the slant. And, of course, I was just playing innocently on this object. It seemed reckless to my parents, yet they indulged all of my whims. My mother would often say how unladylike it was though. But she took great pleasure in my open independence. And my father cherished it all. He was a man very socially advanced for his time. Both saw it as benign play. And, if they had been aware, they would have eventually tolerated the fact that it was actually the youthful purity of a slowly burgeoning consciousness moving towards a natural and mature sexuality.

Today, I use this stationary quality with my cock as she comes up to meet it and cause friction.

Then, noticing the work is being done entirely by her, he begins a very unhurried mimicking of your column in search of my opening. To lengthen the process, she pretends not to quite know where that naughty tool of his is; which, of course, causes her throb to rise at this delay. Finally, she has had enough of that. He discovers her opening. All this while she has raised her nipples to a stage of hurt, hurt, hurt, pleasure by her own mouth.

It was thus then and it is so now. As soon as I grew my breasts big enough to reach, I used that technique often. I always dreamt someone chewing them very delicately and easy, no rush, then firmer and faster. No one has done it like you Juria. I think that may be because you can feel your own nipples response to a woman's mouth and most definitely associate and know. It is rare a man who allows that part of his body to be touched; so sweet a man who finds it delicious.

As my nipples surge, my clit does likewise. I feel an overwhelming need to tend to my clit and set in mind to do so. I switch faster and faster from her to him whilst they lick my radiant tips there.

Thinking of you and things that I would like to spontaneously tell you to do at moments, allow me to tell you lustily, that I am you, tonguing me and yet going beyond that unbelievable point that you give me. The supremely potent waves of spasm that you gave me that one eve, hangs over any completion that I attempt to attain. I always feel and will always feel that blissful and profoundly felt moment was obtained and held for that miraculous length of time that it was maintained for very beautiful and exact reasons; reasons that are probably not duplicable ever again. But I keep trying.

My god it is late! So much gained languorous foreplay, so much lost time. The need to have that area between my legs draw something in is now huge. I first learned this yearning by wanting to follow the natural line of the clit, down the lips, down into a slippery, sliding sensation and then feel inside there. I follow the path of least resistance now as I did when younger. I use my two fingers to dexterously rub, rotate or fill me fully. It penetrates as a cock would. Astoundingly though, much more can also be accomplished with these fingers at my impulse and desire. I have touched there quizzically at first with a feeling of guilt and want in unison. Guilt succumbed to my potent need. I will poke and stroke in a fine tip-like manner at random, which makes my resistance a thing disappearing. Such a delightful disappearance that. Random poking and unknowing stroking, really unexpected attention is one method that brings out a tremendous amount of silken wet-some and a garden of vivid different scents from me, from her. I love it when I can get your organ, Juria, sopping wet up and down from my oral activity and then intensively grind into it as if to force the skin to absorb it. I wish very much that I could have come down on myself today. But once I did permit my fingers to glide magically over and inside of me, I release in a glorious and soaking wet and altogether teasing crying manner. I also do lick it dry. The cock is alternately yours, mine, his, and no one's in particular. It has no size, no genuine qualities of a cock but that it is gentle and brutal at separate moments. I get rascally brutal to make the release; a large amount of force upon bracing force against my burning nub, so constant and at high speed. I can never imagine that you, my dear and sweet Juria, would even feel safe in doing that to me. I will have to show you that it is reasonable. That would be good for both of us.

Juria, god I want you! Solitary games are a joy. Yet finding your real flesh and fine demeanor fulfill me mightiest.

This has been my first session where I strongly took the opposite sex part in searching that explosive apex, a conscious, deliberate enactment. Before, I always knew I wanted to just find grateful release. Either I needed it because of strain or elapsed time or to explore with a highly enticing looking object. But always with pure intention of getting myself to a high pitched place of control lost. That has always been the core of each adventure until now.

This time, I physically took the place of a man, like you, wanting to please a woman, like me.

By this time dear husband and lover of mine, I have managed to work myself up to an overwhelming sensation to rush down and find you laboring over a thick tree trunk, sizing up a safe fall, sitting nicely on the ground, knees hunched, arms clasped around those knees, breeze blowing brightly, clouds allowing no breach to the heavens and take you right then and there. And merely demonstrate my full and ever replenished love for you. This is the sensation that I have as time leaps away this day.

That not to be denied or disguised masculine impulse of mine is so strong in me; that wanting to physically take you perhaps. It is the self same passion behind that extremely sensuous night that I demanded that we leave our clothing on and that gave me such an erotic shiver I had not felt for such a long time. Do not deny it! I love you Juria and I love your body's awareness. If I can at all give to this world a more responsive body, I wish it to be learned with you and the likes of you. Take a long good look at that last sentence and feel a joy. Read it literally again. These would be encounters I shall henceforth be involved in: whether they have my initiation, instigation, my fullness, my shallow attempt, my real happiness, my techniques and my uninhibited flow. All are up to me. This I wish consciously and thoroughly for you to feel too. Also, my concluding need is to be touched by me in a manner unknown and not experienced by you in the pre-me era; thus unique to our love.

Know that I will always want or desire some tangible in-your-own-solid-mind fierce fire.

And that fire awakening no matter where time leads, takes or beckons each of us. For I feel a vivid strength without soft sentiment, knowledge of your body, soul and mind that will expand infinitely and ride and flow in, around and at the core of my brain. It jars my love of life so pleasingly, eternally. Take some more of me.

Now, my lengthy adventure and its associated passion are diminished; but only for the meanwhile, as yours did when you left for the forest so long ago, just this morning. Yet the realization of your presence and your sexual cravings have me enthralled and climbing-a bamboo tree possibly-most of the time; all of the time. My cock, his cock, is stiffening again. I am sure, with you as my companion, that it would remain in that state if it could for a very admirable stretch of time.

I love you my most precious Juria.

Danika."

Chapter 7

Circles

Her senses pricked at her viciously. Her hearing was so acute and on edge that she caught the minutest of whispering acoustic currents. Her sight pierced solid objects and assaulted the darkest crevices until everything in this wood was visible to her. The dark became light to her. She smelled what she wished not to, yet had to in those wafts of odor and scent which preyed at her subtly flaring nostrils. Her brain foretold events that were even now occurring within the perimeters of her terrain; terrain that flooded ever outward into domain of her absolute and unyielding possession. That psychic gift held her in sway; vividly, completely. Images of parents tossed, children lost. The vision began blurred. Then it coalesced into coherent details, frightening details. Not for her frightening, simply for others.

What Viktoria sensed so intensely that it was near to assaulting her every body part was the distant approach of children far away and rushing forward without caution or real plan.

Her senses sparked as if they were lit; yet a brain that sensed so much but was caught in that ultimate paradox between doing damage or giving support as best as she could. She knew what her heart would choose. She also knew what her blood would choose. She was hungry. Her loins evinced that pulsation that would soon goad her toward the beings so mindlessly moving through the forest.

This self-analysis of hers occurred all in a pause that spanned mere seconds. Would she wait for them to come to her? Or would she speed toward them? Her itching, tingling and hungry body said to race to her prey. Her warm and yielding heart said to step closer to them but only as close as to watch for their direction and to care for their safety if needed by them.

She knew that it was Hansel and Gretel who ran recklessly through the woods. She also was aware that those tender children attempted to find their Stepmother. And, she also understood that their Stepmother was caught up in her anger at her husband. But that Stepmother was not so overwhelmed by that anger that she would ever have carelessly wound her way into the night shadows of the heavily timbered forest. Viktoria understood that Claire was not in danger as she had taken the boundary trail that was straight and easily followed, easily followed at least for Viktoria.

She also understood that the children had been hugely impulsive in their fear for their Stepmother. The obvious had not occurred to Hansel and Gretel even as smart as these two children were . . . for minds so young. Their sweet and innocent concern for their Stepmother caused Viktoria to smile.

Viktoria softly, self-confidently, separated large branches and breached the tangles of the thick and lazy underbrush.

As she expected, the children drew deeper into the center of the forest with each forward step. They would need the protecting soon enough, not their Stepmother.

Viktoria also discerned that if Claire had known of Hansel and Gretel's current whereabouts that Claire would be full of dread and have a desire to find them and bring them back to the secure confines of the cottage. But Claire did not know, nor did Juria.

Juria, poor fool, was thoroughly oblivious to any harm lurking. He was enmeshed in his cherished delights regarding his and Danika's' once marriage. Viktoria comprehended how enthralled Juria was at this moment. So enthralled was he with his history that he was unable to focus on any other happening. He was a man deeply engaged and entrapped by the document of his present reading. That was so much so that Claire, in close proximity, flew through the front door of the cottage unnoticed by Juria. He had mind only for Danika. The consequences would be long in their unraveling.

Viktoria's motion was graceful in spite of the impediments that she encountered everywhere. And, if she wanted, she could fly. But she had always hated bats. Such ugly creatures they were. Even vampires have their pride she thought. And then she laughed fully.

But she could not will her hunger away; or that blood yearning for more blood. She had an insatiable appetite for the vibrant red liquid. It smelled so awful though. She was compelled to have it often but the stench afterwards would have made her spew her meal into all corners of any room had she not now been blessed with the vampire's hard stomach and capable nostrils. And she knew how a victim's blood was the only, the only, fluid that pacified the torment of hunger and the ultra-acuity of all of her other sensations when she was thus. It was as an orgasm for her that provided massive release and the most luxurious of relaxation. It was much more than relaxation though; peace and tranquility and the feeling that one was spiritually soothed, cupped in the gently pulsing and softly warm hands of God. Or the universe if there was no God. She knew her hope yet felt her fear there equally.

Slow forward thrust into the overarching firs had occurred automatically. That she could so naturally maneuver past knobby roots, fallen limbs, through bizarre entanglements of vines, over stony encumbrances gave her a rush of ecstatic feeling about her capabilities.

And she feared no living creature, sentient or otherwise, in the forest. Her power was so mighty that all animals instinctively avoided her advance; all those animals on the alert for any adversarial presence, at least. Some animals became careless but never intentionally so. She was on any animal in an instant, tearing at their throat, gulping at their life blood. But the blood of an animal was not like the blood of a human.

The blood of a human was richer, denser, its qualities to satisfy defied an understanding of why. But once tasting the livid liquid all questions as to its effect were shattered and cast away. A vampire didn't care then. Sustenance and satisfaction were all that was important.

The children were closer at hand now. Viktoria's randomly available clairvoyant faculty spat out the fact that Hansel was dropping bread crumbs along their path so as not to become lost. What he had failed to fully consider was the fact that many of those crumbs were being fought over by greedy bird's intent upon their meager meal.

Viktoria sensed their consternation at not finding their Stepmother.

By this time, Hansel knew that he and Gretel were lost as well. He wavered between returning to the cottage, if they could, and forging ahead into the even lesser known arms of the forest. He capitulated and decided to go neither forward nor backward for the moment. He had found a slight stone outcropping that would protect them somewhat. It was the best that he was able to manage for the two of them. He was holding back his tears so as to be brave for Gretel. Gretel kept quietly crying for Claire, then home, then Claire and Juria too. Hansel hushed her and told her that they had to be silent. He didn't want them to become prey through what he imagined would be a harsh night for them. It was cold and they were cold. All Hansel could do was to hold Gretel and allow their bodies heat to heat their edges underneath the two furs and allow them enough to survive. All this was transmitted to Viktoria in an instant.

When Viktoria arrived at the outer margins of the area surrounding the outcropping, she circled the patch of rock and wood quietly but quickly. If there were predators, she would leap immediately. Her heart had overcome her hunger as she knew that she could satisfy both. She would guard Hansel and Gretel's' rough nest while finding game to satisfy her hunger. Her hunger yielded to that as Viktoria's heart was outsize and was all that protected her from becoming simply a set of slashing teeth atop a ravenous appetite.

Her appetite was about to be fulfilled. Viktoria leapt. Her aim was just below the savage glittering eyes and open jaws of the sodden, hairy, huge but emaciated beast.

The beast was a starving, therefore careless, brown bear. He stalked the children. As he stalked, he was unaware of being stalked himself. Viktoria rarely sighted one of these shaggy creatures but here one desperate one was. The bear was in instantaneous shock at the rapidity of her attack. The attack was brutal, monstrous and so efficiently performed. Her teeth lanced through the tough flesh to the pumping pipe that was the bear's vital artery. Viktoria growled. The bear whimpered for just a tick of time. Then it shook its mammoth head. And he howled. He howled so loudly that though well a mile away, Hansel and Gretel heard the roar in their restless dreams. What should have awakened them did not as the children were beyond exhaustion. Viktoria was glad of this even as she was enmeshed in her present battle.

Viktoria slashed at the throbbing artery over and over. Her teeth moved with incredible precision at the mark that would be fatal to the bear. The bear attempted to flee the onrushing teeth that drove deeper into the exposed throat. Viktoria's strength was so brutal and overwhelming that she simultaneously ripped the artery loose and twisted the bears head until the neck cracked horribly. A gush of blood erupted around Viktoria's face. She tossed the bears body on the ground and slaked her thirst with a grim gulping sound. She knew that this had to be done swiftly so that she could return to her protection of Hansel and Gretel immediately. She was fully satisfied.

It was time to go.

Chapter 8

Claire's Angst

Claire abruptly turned on her heels and began the return effort back to the cottage. None of this felt right to her. She and Juria had always supported one another through all oncoming challenges between them. It was gospel that they did that for each other. No one else would. And huge challenges they had had. Like the moment when she and Juria stood in front of her parents . . . together . . . and revealed to them that Claire was going to take her leave from the estate and live as she should with her lover in his cottage. And another huge challenge came when she and Juria had felt the necessity to formalize their partnership into the bonds of marriage which allowed Claire and Juria to rejoice and the world to know of their deep rejoicing. Especially, though, it had shattered her parent's calm and serene shell. They loved her so fully that they did not know how to handle Claire's commitment to a man and an existence that was not shielded for her by fortune and money. They wanted her safe and happy. Not meandering through, what seemed to them, a life of impoverished means and limited opportunities for their daughter, their beloved Claire. Nonetheless, Claire and Juria had married and her parents, especially her father Henry, had begrudgingly attended the beautiful event.

Nothing had lifted her heart more than the ceremony and the life that she now lived with Juria and the children. She would not weaken now and let it become shattered over what amounted to a ghost of the past; a being wonderful and gorgeous but now departed. How could one be so small spirited as to allow a memory of a deceased first wife to wreak havoc on a present and so active love as was theirs? She again smiled openly at those positive memories of Juria. The ripest memory was of him in his wedding attire: so uncomfortable in finery that was not his familiar terrain. But he yielded and made that sacrifice for her and her parents. Her parents had made one and one request only, finally. They had wanted a lavish wedding for their daughter at their estate which, of course, by tradition and their insistence, they paid for. He walked through the ceremony and let his beaming pleasure at their permanent joining take over his spirit. Damn the outer appearances! She knew he had been swollen with love for her as she had been for him. Let the two of them celebrate again. Now! Back up the trail she stepped.

Her steps sounded very hollow and frightening suddenly. Claire had let her focus broaden as the anger whooshed out of her. She felt her aloneness in the dark, punctuated by the mushy sound of those footfalls of hers on the night wet path. Anger was now displaced by a swirl of anxiety... fear even. Fear of the night stalkers of the woods, animals on the hunt for prey. But fear also regarding the words unsaid between her and Juria. And fear multiplied more so by his total immersion into that whatever of Danika's. Claire had not read it so didn't know its contents precisely or what to call it. But the grip it had on Juria was agonizingly obvious to her and would have been to anyone. She had to get back soon. She began to run. Get back woman, back to the cottage.

Young and athletic as she was, Claire had to dodge overhangs, randomly fallen rock and trees with gnarled knuckles protruding out of the dirt. She felt all manner of earthy things reaching up at her to impede her flight home. Her breath came out in panting puffs that immediately formed a visible white in front of her, disappeared though in but an instant. More puffs were replaced with every next strained breath. She began to shiver and her lungs began to ache as if she was being lanced. She was pushed on though by the hand of her fear at her back, that fear which forced her legs to churn and pump, arms to lash fiercely at branches in her way, eyes to parse out the trail in the shroud of blackness surrounding.

The noise she made moving forward was echoing and loud. She knew it but didn't care. Caution was now only a gossamer thread in her mind. Then it was broken entirely in that urgent desire to join back with Juria. She was trying to comprehend her earlier foolishness and what seemed like a terrible overreaction now. But even that receded and blinked out too as she shut thought away and ran, just ran.

She sobbed as she reached the front door of the cottage. Tears held back only because of the stabbing licks of ache and pain in her lungs. She hoarsely gulped for air. No matter all. She was at her doorstep into safety, Juria and the children. She staggered through that entry in exhaustion combined with overarching relief.

Juria found her immediately. He was vividly awake and clasped her to him. He murmured loving words into her hair, her ear, lashes and lips. He was kissing and speaking in a leap frogging jumble of words and breath and touch of his lips. He told her "I turned to explain to you my raptness over Danika's dear writing. To tell you that, though the past is fascinating, it is no longer alive in my mind. My mind holds fire only for you my precious Claire. Ah, only for you my gorgeous one. When I turned from the letter, you were gone. I couldn't imagine and in the middle of the night no less. And I flew to the front door and saw it faintly unclosed. I knew you had gone to the refuge of the woods. But I was also so frightened for your safety and was just ready to undertake my search for you when, magically, you came tumbling through the door into my arms just now. I love you so Claire." The last words repeated in a cascading frenzy at first and then, as moment upon moment had their effect, in gentler and more yielding flow.

Claire felt the joy kindle in her breast at his words. Her retracing back to the cottage had been so the perfect action to take, the right thing to do, the loving thing to do; as she was deeply aware that she loved him fully too.

The cottage was entombed in silence as Claire and Juria simply held the other close, uncertain of the risk of releasing their hold.

Claire, on an impulse, raised eyes to peer at the door to Hansel and Gretel's' bedroom. All was so hushed. Not a stir from that room. Claire drew gently away from Juria. And then she paused, took his hand and led him across the timbered floor to that door. Fulfillment from Juria's embrace made her want to also embrace all in that wonderful household. If not to embrace the children, to disturb them not, at least to look down upon those sweet, sweet children in their innocent, unmoving and soundless sleep was all that she presently desired. She softly curled her fingers around the handle.

There was a cold draft that was sucked out of the bedroom and past Juria and Claire as Claire gazed in at the interior of the small chamber where the children normally slept. The blast of frigidness turned from chill of air to chill of heart. Instant fear roiled into both. Would this night of anxiety and fright ever stop? It was becoming unbearable. The moonlight could be seen shining its luminescence, bursting from the open hole of window. Not just open but wide open. "Hansel, Gretel!" Claire shrieked.

First it was Claire, now it was Hansel and Gretel at risk! Out the window hours ago it would seem from the furiously cold temperature of the room. Claire and Juria were completely baffled. The children had never done this before. Juria stuck his head out the window, strained eyes and ears for clues as to their whereabouts. There was nothing. There was not a murmur from the outdoors . . . as if the surround was waiting expectantly for an action. A foreboding instinct came deeply to the both of them.

This foreboding was much more than palpable. Juria and Claire went out the window as the children had; thrust out the window by virtue of pure forward force.

Chapter 9

Frying Pan's Fire

The wash off of partially dried sticky gore from her reddened chops and bewitching face in the hard surging stream before her occurred rapidly. She splashed hands over her face repeatedly. She did not want to terrify the children any more than they must already be by suddenly appearing drenched in tiny flecks of bear guts and blood in her saving of them. They would be certain to believe their savior was truly not. Viktoria could not, would not have that. She desired their comfort in her rescue of them. And it was time to do just that.

Dawn was not overly far from cracking on the horizon at this moment. Light from sun's rays would be reaching out to the forested land soon enough. And she had to be sequestered in her prison of dirt and wood by then. The children would be up and on foot with the light and warmth of the sun. Her need for speed and finding their forms still huddled in dark's sleep was paramount. She wiped her face then with her sleeves and set off without another moment of delay. She was glad to know that her hot throb was presently satiated too by the massive draughts she had taken from the bear. His life had made hers one she could endure.

Viktoria saw the terror on their faces as she softly approached them. Her psychic abilities were always more muffled and muddied the nearer the sun threatened its presence to her. She was on her own and reliant on her instincts and guile only.

She knelt before them and did not approach further. She reached out a little to them and in the sweetest manner that she could muster-which

34

was very sweet indeed-said "May I help you two as you obviously need that. Where are your parents for God's sake?"

Gretel, being the impulsive good creature that she was immediately trusted this beautiful seeming apparition who was there to show them out of their ghastly predicament. Gretel leaped forward. As she did so, Viktoria stretched her arms out fully to catch a crying, sobbing little girl. Gretel was shivering and shaking fiercely too. "Our Stepmama, we, we haven't found her. She must be lost . . . as we are!"

Hansel lunged for Gretel but was an instant too slow. He caught empty air only as Gretel was already in the arms of the stranger before them. Viktoria saw Hansel's frustration at Gretel's instant trust of her and ensuing outburst of words to her.

Viktoria was absolutely certain that Hansel would follow Gretel, wherever that may be. He would never leave his sister behind. So Viktoria focused on convincing Gretel to follow willingly where Viktoria led. Viktoria was not desirous of forcing the children but would do just that if the time and situation demanded that. And Viktoria's sense was that she wanted to truly comfort the children and have them know that they were genuinely safe in Viktoria's sphere. Now that her bloodlust had been fully slaked, her desire for goodness was fully in command of her motives.

And besides, Viktoria had always, even before her metamorphosis into this darker being, loved children. She would have had ones of her own had she not been changed so early in her life. As a human, she had thought that she had forever to have children. Now she had forever, but not for that.

The lateral corners of Viktoria's orbits turned up as she peered at Gretel. "Gretel, I will see to your safety. Do not fear that. I am a neighbor of your household. And I know these woods very well. I will lead you back to your home. But first I want to warm you and your brother, I presume, at my small but fine home. I will see that you are fed also.

Let us do that now. I can see that you require appropriate and quick shelter."

Gretel was just so scared that she would have followed an offer of comfort and rescue anywhere. Even at the cost of ignoring Hansel's protests. So she was absolutely ready to go where this woman went. Go right now; go before right now. Viktoria read this as if Gretel were shouting it out. So Viktoria held her arms out to Gretel and Gretel melted into them for a moment. Then she seemed to dislodge the cold and whatever minute uncertainty remained within her by shaking her shoulders and trembling briefly.

What she spoke next was so natural at this point. "Yes please. Take us. Come on Hansel, we should go with her. I am hungry. I almost feel faint."

Viktoria was pleased. Hansel was not. He rushed forward and cried to Gretel to come back. Gretel and Viktoria were already walking forward though. And Gretel was oblivious to Hansel's appeals to her.

So Hansel, in his consternation, kept upon their heels. What else could he do? He would not abandon his little sister ever. Viktoria was aware that his pride in himself was at stake without a doubt. That someone so young could also be as mature and wise as Hansel was amazing she believed. His wisdom in following would entrap him though.

Viktoria traveled at a very rapid pace. She had one arm around Gretel's waist and nearly carried her. In that manner, Gretel was able to keep up with Viktoria. Being the agile child that he was, Hansel easily made haste as well.

Viktoria could feel the beginning heat of the morning sun approaching. An hour was probably all that separated her from her own life and death. She had to accomplish a number of tasks before closing the lid of her coffin upon herself to be shielded from the light of day. And she would accomplish those tasks with or without gentleness. Gretel was being more than cooperative. That was excellent. And Hansel was forced to be so. That was excellent too. Viktoria was pleased with events that did not slow her down.

They reached Viktoria's door within moments of Viktoria's prior pleased ruminations. The house that they were about to enter was a sweetly large shelter from the harsh and frigid woods. Gretel would have entered all manner of doors as long as they led her to a warm hearth and the prospect of food to fill her little tummy.

Hansel, obviously, was not so sure of this being to their advantage. It must have seemed more an abduction to him. He would go in though if Gretel did. And Gretel was not about to stop at the entry. Viktoria was not about to allow Gretel to decide anyhow. Viktoria moved with such purpose. Hansel had no choice but to follow and hope that she was true to her word; which was Viktoria's every intention. She smiled at the fact that Hansel felt stymied. It was a long set of hours since the children had laid on their familiar beds preparing for peaceful slumber. Even with Gretel's relief, the young ones frustration was clearly evident to Viktoria.

Enveloped by warm air and delicious smells, all three stood in her kitchen. The children could not know that it was rarely used. This was one of those occasions that made cooking perfect. Viktoria hungered for many things but food was not one of them.

She was a wonderful cook though. She had, especially, learned the art of bread baking long before she was turned. It was such a luscious skill to have. Her taste buds remembered those days as did her nostrils. Memories they would stay though. The baking of this bread was simply for the sake of Hansel and Gretel, no more, no less. And they were hungry. Gretel basked in the aromas without reserve by clapping in delight. Hansel did not. Viktoria heard his stomach growl loudly enough though that Gretel laughed aloud. Hansel appeared chagrined.

Gretel was dancing around in primal happiness that she and Hansel were safely ensconced inside Viktoria's house.

And now she brought that hot, sliced pile of aromatic wonderful bread to the table. Gretel pulled out a chair that seemed to have been placed there just for her. Hansel, in his famished condition, let caution speed away and grabbed his chair too. Once having set the bread down in front of the children, Viktoria brought forth very cold and delicious looking milk in an overfull pitcher. Cups were brought to their brim with the frothy white liquid. The children ate as if there were no tomorrow.

Viktoria had concocted a straightforward plan for the two children. She had virtually no time remaining to lead the children back to their parents; she would surely fall victim to the sun's savage rays if she tried now. So she insured that the children would fill their bellies and then want to sleep the light of day away.

And that is exactly what happened. As they finished their repast, their small heads began to nod. Viktoria drew them to a little extra bedroom in the corner of the house and tucked the children in to the one bed. They were oh so happy to be led to that bed. Their furs were placed over them by Viktoria. In moments, Hansel and Gretel were sound asleep. The vampire closed the door so softly and locked that door from the outside.

The children would go nowhere now. Hopefully they would not even awaken before her awakening.

Chapter 10

Dreams Unfolding

Clack. Then clack again. She snapped the inner coffin lock bars into place. The earthy smell of soil surrounded her. Would she ever find comfort and peace while entombed this way? Yet she had to yield to the weird paralysis of daytime sleep that was demanded of her, dark being that she would forever be.

The musty fingers of dirt's odor were penetrating through nose to brain. Her nose detested it; her brain was anesthetized by it. Soon she would be vastly unconscious. Dreams would suffuse her entire world in light speed moments. Here was the one place where her wild, unruly and vivid images did not immediately have to be fed by blood or release after!

Absurdly total silence played off the inner surfaces of her coffin. Neurons inside her head fired off at a miraculously fevered pace though.

If images could somehow be mysteriously morphed into light and sound, an orchestra would now be in crescendo with heads bent closely to their instruments and the maestro gripped in a seizure of directed movement.

Above the pit, where the collage of coordinated sound emanated from, was a stage. It was a primitive stage. Upon that stage, dancers swirled and drove their legs and their slipper sheathed feet toward a message of strength yet grace and purity. The sinuous and delicate clash of the dancer's motion blended into what should have been oppositional but instead were perfectly composed and coordinated. Ultimately this tableau was a paean to the notion that strength and delicacy could be wonderful partners.

Why though was there a blur to the dancer's solidity? And why were there wavering shifts in their shape and motion? And there she was suddenly in the midst of those very dancers. Somewhere, deep toward the core of her mind, Viktoria knew that she was locked in a dream. It was a dream of parts fantasy and unreality and then parts of her true earlier life. She appeared as she had been on that other side of her being; the time before this infinite trap of hers had begun.

Beauty she was. And she shimmered and undulated as if she was a mirage seen in high heat at a distance. The moments of solidity showed a wondrously slim form of leaping and then balancing appendages of the monstrously capable dancer that she had been. Even with her mask on, her astounding look and gorgeous glow sent sparks into the audience.

Body held fast by forces darker than her will and desire could control, Viktoria knew that the dream was infinite and covered terrain of her past. The tendrils of her conscious mind disappeared again into the lavish tapestry of her long ago experiences. She had been an aspiring and then very successful dancer once. Oh, that once upon a time could be again and therefore lives remade!

The Maestro was an imposing figure. He had a big body, a handsome face with long hair flying back but was also an artiste, a connoisseur of music and drama. He was a consummate expert at handling the violin so dexterously. Such a sensitive touch that man had.

His aspect made her wet even while she concentrated on her poses, her steps, her enmeshment with her character. After all, she was an actress even more than she was a dancer. She, like him, excelled at so much. And he, with so many other passionately pressing admirers, always chose her. They were mutually mesmerized by one another. Even as the dream of him, of them, would loosen and would begin to recede and lose form, her loins, her pulse there was liquid and hammering her desire into a flaming shape. That shape would eventually engulf her completely. Now though, the dream dominated with the pulse secondary.

This Maestro was, as well, a famous composer of both plays and opera. He could write, he could direct, he could conduct, he could sing his own creations, or take a part in anything theatrical. The world was at his behest . . . but he wanted her. She was enthralled by this fact.

Was the dream making more of him than he actually had been? Did she or the dream care? No, they absolutely did not! She had loved him greatly and so, to her, he was the greatest of men.

Her paralyzed and entombed form felt the heat of the dream in breast, belly and between her thighs.

The dream was transporting her into a scene that had shaken her and transformed her beyond the believing.

She and this man were enlivened by each other's touch. He was suckling at one thoroughly sensitive and aroused nipple of hers. His hands swept over her dancer's garments. They were nearly removed and only tights remained on her. He was fully clothed though but lusted and hungered for her large mounded chest that she so desperately gave to him. She gripped his hair with a hand and pushed his head deeper into her urgent flesh. His lips drew her nipple into his mouth through the thin top of her tights. Then he paused. She panted while he tore at that top and pulled it down to her waist. She removed it the remainder.

The room was backlit by a blazing fireplace fire. It was warm. The fire and the warmth enlarged. The heat and crackle were overtaking the dream. But the dream would not yield yet. She and he were still fused to one another. He now had fingers touching her molten liquid there, spreading her slickly, subtly sticky nether lips. Her pulse was raging now.

Body or dream, she couldn't tell the source. But source be damned as it was an astounding sensation, one that devoured her. Or was it he who devoured her! Oh my God! He was suddenly at the carotid pulse of hers, kissing that pounding artery at her neck. Then she felt a minutely lancing pain at that precise location. She could hear his gasping breath. She knew not what was happening but succumbed utterly to his gulping of her blood. No matter how much blood that he drained from her, her pulse never ceased. The exploding throb felt mighty; heaven sent but also thrusting her hell bound. And yes, before the flame fully penetrated the dream, she knew that she would let him taste of her over and over.

She was awake now. The dream, how long ago had it ended? Time was out of her reach as she raised her eyelids. But just for a fleeting moment as she realized that when the dream occurred was of minor importance in comparison to what the dream signified. She had loved him. She had willingly surrendered her heart to him. She had made herself so vulnerable to his passion and guidance. And, at first, she had thought his gift to her a product of their love.

As she gained a cynical wisdom over time though she realized that it was a simple reflex of his to drink her blood. He had hungered for her but had never loved her. It was a hated bit of knowledge. It must have been her trusting love that touched him enough for him to have spared her a death as he raped her jugular. So she was bestowed the gift of the vampire. And so it shall be for all of her eternity. Clack; clack as she unsnapped the lock bars to the coffin.

Chapter 11

Pressing On

The edge of panic was palpable for Claire and Juria. How should they proceed now that they were out the cottage's bedroom window? Juria paused for the moment to let his senses adjust, especially his vision. The panic and heavy rapid heartbeat quite interfered with his ability to attempt to pinpoint Hansel and Gretel's direction. Claire was uncertain as to Juria's momentary stillness. She wanted to press on without hesitation, not even for a whit. But she absolutely trusted Juria's acumen in tracking through the foreboding and unforgiving tangle of trees that thickly surrounded the cottage. So, from behind, she simply placed a waiting hand on his still arm; a statues tableau.

Juria placed himself in Hansel's mind as best he could. Where would Hansel suspect that Claire would have gone if not the perimeter path? Juria turned abruptly and took Claire's chin in his hands. "Claire, tell me where you would have walked if the simple choice of the perimeter path had not occurred to you?"

Claire's thoughts had run parallel to Juria's as it turned out. And she knew exactly where she would have gone. Hansel and Gretel, long ago, had shown her a smooth step of hard stone on the forest verge. Once the branches were parted there, a zagging trail of sorts appeared. Juria was aware of that easier trek through the initial overhang of forest border. Yet, he was uncertain if Claire knew and whether the children were also aware of that fact . . . if it was a fact at all. He needed Claire to speak. And she did. "Juria, that stone that the children showed me once. They were so proud to have done that."

43

Claire was about to say more but Juria spun round and sped toward the trees. Claire leaped forward with Juria.

Juria held tree limbs apart for Claire. They stepped into the densely enclosed feel of forest. There was the full orb of the moon overhead. Its gleam though was almost fully obscured by the nearly impenetrable coniferous canopy. Maybe a very light dusting of moonlight was scattered here and there along the trail. They would have virtually no help from above. Juria and Claire were absolutely on their own in this search for Hansel and Gretel.

Fortunately, Juria wore the forest like a second skin. He loved it, he lived it. Now he would be forced to reveal his expertise. And he hoped that his skills would be enough. Claire and the children were completely relying on it.

The very first sign of the children's presence in the area was several out of place breadcrumbs. The two or three that Juria sighted were partially mashed under one of the stepping stones. One of the crumbs looked unsuccessfully pecked at. Whatever bird pecked at the slightly moist and spongy material was not able to dislodge the crumb from the rock crevice. Juria realized that it was misplaced here, probably dropped by a human hand. Hansel was so very smart! He had done this in order that he and Gretel could find their way back to the cottage.

Juria also understood that Hansel had possibly forgotten how hungry and determined birds would eat or carry those crumbs away. Juria had been very fortunate that any crumbs remained at all. Since these several had, he was certain that the children had entered here.

Juria and Claire then plunged into the narrow, sparsely rocky trail. Juria was acutely focused on any and all signs pointing the way toward the obviously lost Hansel and Gretel. Their anxiety and helpless fear for the children propelled them through the tangled undergrowth that had, through the years, become a severe and impeding overgrowth. The smudges on several of the stones were from the dirt being smeared as

Hansel and Gretel scrambled through here. Juria knew it. And further, ah wretched luck, he knew they were without their shoes in this strong cold.

These signs were so difficult to find in the nearly nonexistent moon glow. He was also on the hunt for bent grass blades, broken flower stems, anything, as the trail began to vanish in the forest's maw. Juria was prodding his mind hard to come up with possible safe havens for the children to shelter.

Claire was behind Juria, yet at his shoulder every moment. She danced in hope, fear and anticipation at each one of Juria's intermittent halts. This was a dance where he led and she followed; as night followed day to be sure. She knew that Juria would use his vast skills and experience-honed instincts to find the innocents: their brood, his blood, so in peril!

Juria froze in place. Visibility spread as moonlight began to give way to dawning sunlight. They had been in flight, their search, for many hours. Frustration pierced them over and over. Tiny cries of hope arose from them at any sign of the children's presence as they continued tracking. Claire whispered to him as he rigidly paused.

"What?"

"See there, an outcropping. Perfect for where they must be! Hansel, Gretel" he shouted, careless of making their presence known. He heeded nothing now but his desire to hold his children close to his breast, safe and sound.

Nothing. Once his shouts died, a quiet so deep was all that surrounded them in return. The silence was so overwhelming that both Juria and Claire felt as if they were being suffocated in it.

Juria and Claire stumbled to that outcropping wildly. Juria pulled up and scanned the overhang intensively. They had been here. Fur fibers, thank God, for this told him they still had their blankets with them, minutely flecked the ground. They both passionately prayed for the children to be nearby.

Find them was all that thumped at their minds.

Chapter 12

No Sanctuary

Juria could not help his crushing fright at the potential death of his children. He had already faced that with Danika unexpectedly. And now that could happen to Hansel and Gretel. This thought caused his chest to ache and heart to briefly spasm.

And he had agonized when he had become aware of Claire's absence tonight also. What if he had lost her as well? His mind was seized with the knowledge that there was no sanctuary from sudden deprivation. He was consciously aware of its inevitability generically but was always overwhelmingly shocked when its specter treaded upon his own doorstep.

Ironically, having Claire so close to him now made him inwardly tremble at her potential loss juxtaposed with why their pleasures together meant so much to him. Strangely, at this time of search and anxiety, his mind became automatic.

His mind automatically guided his senses, his feet and his keen ability to find the children. Simultaneously, his mind was driven to pictures of sensual events of his and Claire's. A bombardment of erotic images arose. It provided him an enormous distraction from all else. He had to manage relief from his abundant anxiety somehow!

A strong image pastime commanded his mind, an image that he had absolutely no immediate control over.

The children were safely with Henry and Adelaide in estate's fold. Juria and Claire had taken this opportunity to seek out their favorite stream at plateau base. The cutting splash, running flow and sparkling crystalline changes of rain added wild water rushed by them in fresh splendor. They had just stepped through a patch of slender fir to stream's edge where they sat contentedly.

Juria took Claire's hand and then they both were still.

Claire broke the quiet and braved the shimmering liquid by dipping her toes into its quick wash past her. She wiggled those toes in the frigid substance so as to keep her digits from bluing and freezing. The water continued its cold caress and Claire resisted removing them. Juria was mindful of her playfulness.

Her glowing quality surrounded him; he was perpetually captivated by this in her. She lifted her dripping, now glacial toes to his lips. He kissed and sucked them warm again. Pink climbed back into them with Juria's effort. She lay back as Juria tended further to those toes.

The sun was intense and enveloping. A breeze dispelled the high noon heat and turned it into a soothing, blissful blanket wrapped around them. He stayed the course by playfully kissing her smooth textured skin of ankle, calf, then impishly, her thigh. He moved his fingers ever nearer juncture of legs and then leaned over her and brushed his lips over and over the round of both of her thighs. Juria's center began to tighten as arousal inserted itself into their games.

Claire stroked his hair easily and he felt the soft parting flow of it. Her flesh was petal scented. Juria kissed her juncture through her undergarment and his excitement flared as his lips tingled with her heat and moisture there. Claire spread her legs further for him to nuzzle more deeply. His balls and expanding cock were fraught with increasing tension. He raised his fingers to her nipples then and they coursed and thickened with blood. Her mount wetted considerably at that moment.

Claire sweetly pulled at Juria's hair so that he sat in front of her with his legs curled beneath him.

She revealed her desire to him by placing her fingers over the hardening circle of his cock which bulged against his garb; she squeezed the outline of his spongy column over and over. Juria undid his fall front and Claire reached in and pulled his thick shaft, head first, out through the opening. He comprehended that she was rather enamored of first view of his tender cockhead. It was suffused and red and magnetically inviting to her.

She took her thumb and index finger, creating a complete circle over his glans only, to and fro from back ridge to forward tip. Then she grabbed his shaft with her other hand and clenched hard. His glans became hugely swollen as she continued her circle dance upon it.

It was too much for Juria and he removed her from his shaft, at least, so as not to release right then and there.

Claire was no longer capable of sitting motionless. She freed herself from contact and stood before him. She unabashedly removed all her clothing and let it tumble haphazardly.

Juria replaced his fingers upon her hard nipples. He pinched them tenderly and her cleft was saturated. Claire grasped his shaft with one hand, spread her lips and guided him into her depths. She was impaled deliciously; pumped up and down definitely. Juria swelled to proportions he did not know of before this occasion.

Both held their breaths as their motion stopped altogether.

Juria worked Claire's thick and lengthening nipples over with combined gentle twists and fingertip compressions. He was not able to resist cupping her mounds and sucking her there as well. Her moans intensified with the ongoing alternations in stimulation.

Claire hugged him with her legs around his waist. This threw her chest upwards and towards Juria. As he leaned back to view them, his was a sense of large breasts arching upward to take on an even larger appearance.

She seemed to automatically lift her buttocks and fulcrum using her legs for leverage and balance in order to ride him with ever increasing vanishing restraint. Then she placed palms flat to the ground, leaned away and drove herself onto him nonstop.

Juria removed a hand from one of Claire's nipples and started to caress her inflamed bud of concentrated pleasure. As Claire jockeyed over his cock, Juria took hold of her clit barely between two fingers and let her motion move his fingers top to bottom on her sheathed bud. The united sensation of nipple touch, cock swell penetrating her deeply, greed of clitoris with finger touch, all coalesced.

She ratcheted up the speed and vigor upon his length.

Juria was well aware that the confluence of sensation from breast, to clit, to her Venus vault instigated a shivering tension in her. Juria's glans was assailed with her humming interior vibrations; that shiver passed from exterior to interior. Juria's excitement stormed him even as he remained stationary. He had nearly reached his threshold. He panted in short, sharp exhalations. He groaned out to her, "I am, oh yes, going to come, my love!"

Claire's inner flesh expanded and gloved his instrument even more intensively. Movement was so thick and rapid that it was as if they were fused and immobile.

Wave from breast to abdomen, up from thigh and hip crashed together at her core. The waves of delight and joy that Claire repeatedly underwent annihilated his ability to contain himself. Her spasms triggered his explosion into her. He thudded with white heat and blowing starbursts of pearly semen that saturated her. She was bathed in his liquid love. Claire cried out. They absorbed their passion with eyes wide open and were amazed at the sheer bliss of it.

Juria touched her under her left breast and nipple. Their hearts were strong, rapid, synchronized.

Suddenly, from behind, Claire stumbled. The present swam around him.

And he knew that their search had proved thus far fruitless. He spun quickly to assist Claire back up. She was unhurt but supremely frustrated. She reinforced what he knew when she punched out the words "Where are they!"

Desperation compounded. Juria had no better idea of next steps than Claire did.

Chapter 13

Ripped Beyond Recognition

Viktoria's intense dreaming had slowed her for sure. The darkness that surrounded her as she elevated from her sarcophagus was thicker and more pronounced than she was accustomed to. Her waking thoughts were cloudy and indistinct. Her only clear awareness was that all was a tick off, a fraction askew. But how could that be? She was ambulatory and moved her limbs with only a bit of stiffness. The children were secured in the additional room by the outside door lock. She would guide them back to their panicked parents in a short span of time. Certainly, even Hansel could not protest Viktoria's willingness to lead them to their beloved home.

But the dreaming left a remnant, a barrier that blocked her psychic ability and left a naked throb at her temples. The fractional pain there threaded its tight wire from one side of her head to the other.

She, as usual, was craving sustenance upon her daily resurrection from the damp and awful enclosure that her coffin was. She stifled her hunger though as she was determined that the children's safe return would be accomplished before she was overtaken by that crushing need to satisfy herself. It was rolling towards her rapidly in spite of her plans. The remedy for success was speed. By now, she was moving fluidly and was fully able to swiftly make her way to the children's room.

What! She flew to the hole that had been the bedroom door. What had not allowed her to foretell this? Was it her mental labor over the content of her dream that had waylaid her? The door, what remained of it, had been entirely ripped from the door frame and was lying in splinters on the floor nearly beyond recognition. She was not even able to spot either the door handle or lock anywhere within her line of sight. There was only that gaping hole bordered with timber shards where the door had hung.

She was paralyzed in utter shock and dismay. She had so terribly wanted to hand over the children to Juria and Claire this night. Now she could not and had to find out what had become of Hansel and Gretel.

Outrage surged in a burst within her. She was so angry at the audacious interloper for putting the children at risk and having had the bravado to have diminished her sense of self and belongings. This vile invader would meet her face to face. Of that she was absolutely determined to have happen. Viktoria would love that encounter, the sooner the better. She was also so aggravated with herself. She had failed as the powerful being that she always desired to see herself as. That sense had been not just pricked but annihilated. She had to recoup herself and gather the children back to her bosom.

She squeezed her eyes tightly shut and furiously focused her thoughts down to a picture of Hansel and Gretel in the captivity of this other being. Or was it more than one involved? She was aware of the forward moving power of a group together, intent upon certain actions, vague and ill-defined to Viktoria even as she intensified her concentration.

Viktoria could not push through to visualize present events surrounding Hansel and Gretel. It was as if there was a dark energy pressing against her access to her inner panorama. Over and over, Viktoria evoked Hansel and Gretel's images. And, repeatedly, those images would vividly form and begin to coalesce into a coherent scene. Then all shimmered momentarily, shook for but a fraction too. Then an explosion of those embodiments into brightly colored molecules would escape into the fringes of her mind. After, the image fuzzed and turned black.

Damn, she thought, this can't be.

Even in her rage and welter of confusion, she was wise enough to give up this approach to her problem's solution. She was not enamored of futility. When she felt stymied, she easily switched to other avenues. So she snapped her eyes open. And, even in the midst of wanting to repair or, at least, neaten the carnage of property before her, she had to find those children. Correcting the fact that she and her belongings had been savaged had to come later.

Yet she was so hungry too. But if she could capture the beast who had absconded with the children, she could resolve all, even her hunger. She could taste the sluicing blood pouring down her throat as she fantasized the killing that was sure to come. It made her pulse heavily throughout her vital sexual organs. She moaned and was helpless in touching her nipples. She stroked them because she had to. The urgency there was compelling. The sensation of her soft thick nipples stirring and growing hard and firm was delicious and hypnotizing. She did all of this through her clothing. The material was soft and thin. Her very full and large breasts threw those nipples into her reaching fingers.

She broke the automatic reaching and turned sharply to rush through the front of her cottage.

She forced herself to sooth the throb by fixing on the idea of rescue and revenge. She felt her confidence and strength returning. She thrilled to that; her muscles bunching; her blood hurling through her vessels, her sex drenched, her senses acutely elevated and her entire body in luscious desire for the hunt.

The wild excitement of her pursuit was what gripped her as she leapt into the woods. Strangely, there were no footprints, no evidence of entry in or exit from her abode at all. That rattled and perplexed her. The entire episode had done that as it had been a jumble of overwrought feelings, a stubborn inability to psychically view the children, a swirl of hungry sensation and a lurching back to confidence in her abilities.

She had felt all too human, disabled and unnerved. The relief was sweeping over her as she recovered her balance as a dark being; the dark being who carried power and animal certainty so readily and easily. That dark being told her that there was no doubt about her control and domination over others. Viktoria had not a trace of ambivalence about that unique capability. For her, that was an addiction to savor.

Her search was not going to be thwarted. She ruled this terrain. She wanted never to question that again.

Chapter 14

Encounter Beyond Comprehension

Back turned, attention focused, Juria was unaware.

Claire absolutely was not. She was transfixed by the spectacle that enlarged by the moment to blot out the sky's moon. Claire knew that she had never been rooted to one spot before. It was a literal and emotional petrification. She was stone and fascinated, mindless and functionless. Acute fear, terror gripped her completely.

Claire's pupils were huge.

Black upon black, the dark sky darker, internal turbulence matched external turbulence as the currents of air surrounding the creature's wings were beaten into whooshes of sound. Claire shivered as she watched the oncoming silhouette that seemed to suck all the moonlight to it where the light then streamed into the creature's chest to disappear as if into a greedy, clutching black void.

Claire felt an encompassing sensation then, a sensation that vibrated and grew as the image of this winged thing grew. It was a vibrating and a tingling that subtly began to assault her loins. She imagined that she was shaking her head in a hard "No!" over and over and shrieking "How can this be!" as her head remained frozen and only her pupils changed in size. She knew that she must scream at Juria but could not. This looming overarching form held her totally as it approached.

Juria must have turned by now to behold the forward rush of the enormous bat. But Claire was not certain of anything except that she was

56

bound in chains by ungodly, unholy happenings; incomprehensible, especially the excitement pressing and churning between her legs.

The bat vanished instantly as it touched the solid earth and became a much less disturbing form, though with ominous aura nonetheless; threatening because of what Claire had just witnessed and because of what continued to gather and swell sexually in her. She detested the latter but was overwhelmed and mystified by the eroticism of the moment. She should be in absolute fear and trembling.

Claire felt Juria's rasping breath at her neck.

Juria was spellbound and rigid behind her, rapt and not stirring except for his respirations.

Was this shape shifter the same vision for Juria as for her? It must be a woman he saw also as Claire felt his cock climb and pulse against her buttock. He had to be as stunned by his flaring cock as she was by her steady fluttering of tantalizing heat seated deeply in her vault. She wanted to touch herself, touch Juria, and touch the vision before her.

A soft, assured smile broke across the apparition's face. Her eyes were alight with an inner burning glow; such radiant and piercing irises that bade obedience from Claire and Juria. And obey they would.

There was a seething energy emanating from the woman, an energy that felt like a furnace needing to be fed, to be fueled. As her energy mounted so did Claire's, so did Juria's. Claire had not felt Juria's cock so massive ever before. Strangely, Claire was not offended by Juria's response. Claire was equally as desirous.

The woman advanced very slowly. As she did so, her teeth became prominent, especially two tiny scimitars revealed as her smile enlarged. She halted then, smile collapsing, face a welter of confusion suddenly.

Again she morphed radically. Grotesque bat form exploded off the ground back into the night!

Claire was shocked by the instantaneous disappearance. All sexual pulse died as blood drained from her face and fright recaptured her. The pressure of Juria's cock against her clothing relaxed precipitously until his tube was not felt at all.

The woman's sexuality and beauty would not leave Claire's mind. The woman literally smoldered. She had been garbed in sheer flowing garments that could not have warmed her at all. No matter as it was obvious to Claire that the woman was oblivious to the cold and damp forest.

Claire's image of this woman was thus: Her height was not out of the ordinary, although the energy pouring from her made her height seem extraordinary; she was lean as if her molten fires inside consumed her; had long raven hair that perfectly matched the deep color of nipples and aureoles on her large mounded ebony breasts; a sharply etched face with the fullness of lush eyebrows, the elongated length of lashes, and the wonderfully positioned and proportioned cheekbones to constitute what all, certainly Claire, would call a beauty sublime. Claire had been hypnotized by her flattened belly, sweet and supple contours of hip, leading most likely to deliciously turned buttocks. And finally, there were her visibly strong and long lean legs. It was a picture of especial eroticism for Claire.

Claire had to find out Juria's reaction to what had just transpired; other than his very apparent momentarily swollen cock.

Claire forced her body away from the now empty spot before her, swiveled her neck slightly and locked eyes with a breathless Juria. Both of his cheeks were livid and blotched with ghostly shades of white surrounding. He was equally in shock with Claire and his visage showed every millimeter of that.

They held on to one another fiercely. Then Claire turned torso to torso with eyes still locked on his. Claire whispered as best as she could, "Good God Juria, what did we just apprehend? I am weak with fright!"

She spoke nothing to him of being weak with desire as well.

Juria roused himself and Claire attended to every word, every tonal nuance that fell from his lips. "It was an apparition, was it not?" Claire could make out the tiny tremble in his utterance.

"It flew to us, and then became woman. And, oh god, winged creature again! This cannot be! I won't believe it! You love, what did you perceive it to be?"

His eyes searched hers in the hope that she had an answer that worked for him.

Claire was utterly relieved to know that Juria and her visions were identical; either they were both crazy or the vision before them had just been confirmed as real. Claire had always been well wedded to reality, Juria also. Reality it had to be then!

Claire pushed out these words to Juria, "Yes my darling that was exactly as I saw and experienced it. I am so scared for us all; for you, me, the children."

Though astounded by these swirling and raging contradictory feelings of hers, Claire perceived without a shard of doubt that she must encounter this woman again.

Chapter 15

Returning Apparition

Smitten with desire, a desire for hot and lush blood, Viktoria shed her wings and fronted Claire and Juria with distinct menace.

Her radiance, at its height during the height of her hunger, was palpable and vast. Human victims kneeled before her needs when she reached this stage of want. Her hot pulse first transfixed those she targeted prior to her feeding, then it pressed them down upon a knee with neck proffered.

Juria and Claire were now to follow in that common pose while she sucked passionately. Claire and Juria, ahhhh yes. She twitched then, she halted then.

Oh my god, it was Juria and Claire!

She was here to lead them to Hansel and Gretel if she could.

Her pulse withered and her face collapsed in confusion as contradictory forces railed in opposition at her core. Her primitive force yielded to her even stronger caring force; this caring force of hers had incredible energy; enough energy, at least, in this second, that she was ripped from the howling blood call.

She shifted back into her wings and shot away rapidly; so afraid was she that she would succumb to the hungry fist clawing through her guts and loins.

That was nearly disastrous for Viktoria. She cherished the possibility of assisting the couple with finding their kin. She desperately had to prove her good heart to herself, that selfsame good heart that had been her trademark of her youth. Sating hunger upon them would have slaked that engine of blood need, yet would have devastated her sense of recreating that ability to be a righteous being.

Hunger mounted as miles gave way to the obsessive power of her flight.

She had to suckle a human this time. Nothing else would satisfy. And she would find it and have it; just not Juria or Claire though. That was absolutely critical.

Also, she lusted for someone superbly handsome or succulently beautiful.

Tonight, for Viktoria, was no routine eve. Her appetite was enormous and she was only ravenous for blood beyond doubt. It had to be blood of a singularly special person; be that of singularly good looks, high status, great political power or fantastic wealth.

She honed her focus down to pinpoint energy. All of her senses supported her present hunt. Her throb was so intense that it was a knot of delicious pain. This throb goaded her on in a controlled frenzy.

Below her, a personal coach was rapidly clattering over a small wood slated bridge. The noise caught Viktoria's attention immediately. She didn't even have to conjure up the small details of the coach to understand the status of the individual seated inside. The polish and shine of the well maintained carriage struck her instantly. And instantly, she was well aware that her prey was perfect, exceptional in one way or another.

Down she plunged, wings slowed to land accurately onto the driver's shoulder. He glanced; he shrieked and fell to the side in a faint.

Viktoria had no intention of taking this man's life. His blood did not compel her enough to make her care.

She wrenched the reins from his still fists though and pulled the horses to a grinding halt. She had changed her shape again; and her feminine form beat with beauty, glitter and demand.

Before the high born male inside could even utter a word, she had opened and closed the carriage door so that she was nestled next to this man. No matter his wealth which resonated in his coach and clothing, no matter his youthful long dark locks and starkly attractive face which could not be hidden in his briefly terrified stare, he was quickly a prisoner of the gleam streaming from her eyes. As she locked his eyes to hers, she gently laid her hand between his legs. This was her foreplay and she had to have that too.

Her lust made her blood lust so much the better.

As her fingers cupped his bulge there, he performed upon her mindlessly, robotically but with lust for her equal to her lust for him. His hands kneaded her head beneath her thick, glowing hair. His breathing was hushed but slightly labored with his motion upon her.

His cock was responding to their simultaneous strokes strongly. He ran his fingers from her smooth stranded hair down to her ass, each of his digits creating its own story as he wove them over her rounded and softly pliant ebony cheeks there. His breath was more ragged as each touch occurred. She was also further stirred by the rousing touch.

And she was yet stirred by his bulging cock shadow which pressed upon the cotton material of his stylish breeches.

Impatient, she simply slashed the material away and freed his very heavy hard length from its entrapment.

She delighted in the motion of his fingers upon her and of her hand now upon him. She tore at her sheer fabric with her other hand and it gave way without resistance. Her voluminous breasts poured toward him. His cock pounded at this sight. Her breasts were wonderfully pendulous and these curves drew his eyes down to her generous dark hued aureoles. Her even darker, thick and long nipples made his appetite soar.

He yielded to his hot desire for her and kissed those swollen tips of hers avidly. He tongued one and strummed the other nipple desperately.

She encircled his drumming cockhead with her thumb and forefinger and rhythmically stroked up and down. She spread his clear dew leaking from his opening over that opening and his crown.

She grazed her lips over his nipples. She understood its effect on men. And, as expected, his moans increased and his big shaft moved spasmodically with each tongue stroke of hers.

He had one barely protruding vein that was placed the entire length of his cock, from base to base of crown. She rubbed it lightly. His gorgeous pulse was easily felt this way. Now though, she wanted to grasp that pulse and feel the entire shaft in the palm of her hand. So she fisted his hard thickness and pumped him; slowly to begin, then faster as she and he lost control.

Her deep urges commanded her, especially as he spread back her flooded vaginal lips and traced over her clit. He thrust several of those fingers into her. She clasped his cock tightly as she stroked over his cock with abandon. Her eyes, her countenance, glazed as his cock thickened and reddened. He was about at his threshold of restraint.

Her hips jerked in quick snaps over and over upon his embedded fingers. He tensed and trembled. She felt a rising pressure between her legs. In wild throated moans, his spurts surged in long pearly jets of come. Viktoria was beyond help; her passion and appetite consumed her. Wave upon wave of release flew to her loins. Her thighs crashed together. And then she drove fangs into his neck. The proffered jugular was pounding and ready for her. She lanced in and gorged herself upon him.

She found his handkerchief at his wrist, powdered and all. She used it to wipe the crimson from her lips and jaws. She was fully satisfied now and was aware that the driver would awaken but the Gentleman never would. She transformed herself after she performed this bit of hygiene upon herself.

Appetite firmly conquered, Viktoria could now return to Claire and Juria without concern.

And she found the two of them as they were attempting to retreat from the forest even without finding Hansel and Gretel.

With raiment's restored with each transformation, Viktoria knew that she, as female, would reapproach them, give them succor and dissolve their fear. She was primed to assist them with the search. They would only treat her as a returning apparition briefly.

Chapter 16

Altogether Now

If she could put them at ease rapidly, she would. Viktoria was aware that this was not to be. The process of bringing Claire and Juria into comfort and relaxation with her would prove to be a rigorous challenge.

Viktoria's naivety, to wish that two civilized individuals would feel trusting after witnessing her transformation from bat to female and back, now female a second time, was absolutely ridiculous. Viktoria had to force vicious control over herself to not double up in raucous laughter at this.

She sought their comfort and would eventually achieve it but saw no glimmer of anything but fear in their faces. Fortunately, Viktoria was calm and did not worry this wrinkle as she had just gorged.

None of her harder vampire edges were presently revealed.

Viktoria approached Claire first.

The woman was obviously weakened from the shock of the Vampire's presence, her powers, and her beauty. These facets of Viktoria's were exactly what she would use to pacify the couple.

Viktoria desired only to link up with them in order to locate and take the children from whatever beast now possessed them. The compelling issue for Viktoria in the immediate moment was to convince the woodcutter and his wife that her beast was actually beauty.

Beauty was about to mingle with beauty as Viktoria stepped steadily in the direction of Claire.

She felt Juria's wary stare upon her too.

Yet, for their alliance to be successful, Claire had to be the gateway: as Claire went so went Juria . . . . within reason.

Besides, Viktoria was stirred utmost by Claire's unconsciously firm stance even when so afraid as this. Her exquisite and flushed good looks drew Viktoria also; drew her so strongly that she had to vividly concentrate to draw breath evenly the nearer she was to them.

Finally, Viktoria, in a gesture very foreign to her, looked down demurely.

Upon raising her gaze back to Claire, Viktoria quickly said this "Claire and Juria, I presume. I want your children safe and well, as you do. I found them lost earlier. I fed them; then I let them sleep as they appeared absolutely exhausted. I left them briefly to tend to my own needs, I am sorry to say. In my short absence, they disappeared. Disappeared is a poor choice of word. Rather, they were taken. My locked door to the room within which they slept was shattered so completely that only splinters of wood remained of it. I was in utter dismay. I searched for them immediately and my search has been far reaching, yielding nothing; until I came across the two of you that hour ago. I would have spoken but had to leave because my needs, once again, had to be fulfilled. You will understand this in me as time passes. It is obvious that your foray into the woods for them has been fruitless as well."

Viktoria could not help her rushed speech as she wanted to make haste in continuing with locating Hansel and Gretel.

Claire seemed emboldened by her sympathetic statement enough to reply, "Would you help us find Hansel and Gretel really? You would not harm us or them. You seemed so horrible in form upon our first view of you! Should we, can we, trust you?"

Claire's desperation sank heavily into Viktoria. "You have powers that we don't. But if you are sincere, guide us as best as you can. Please! Quickly!"

Juria spun his wife around to face him. He exclaimed, "Claire, we have no choice but to trust her. Haste is paramount. The children have to be found and found as soon as possible!"

Juria then gave Viktoria a withering glance that she allowed to ricochet around and past her. "You are superhuman, that we know from our vision of you. But we have our ways also. Know that. Now lead. We are in this together. Hansel and Gretel must be saved!"

Viktoria nodded her assent as she appreciated the couple's predicament.

Little did they realize that they could trust Viktoria in this hunt now shared. Viktoria was livid at whomever had dared snatch the children from her, from her home.

Her other fortress had also been breached by this interloper; her confidence had been shattered and had to be restored. And the children had to be secured as well and returned to Juria and Claire. Viktoria ignored Juria's warning and, as she seethed at her forfeiture and degradation, she rotated and then strode forth.

They followed her closely. All three were attuned to clues to be had amongst the overhang, the dense foliage and the uncut lumber hugging them.

Viktoria completely acknowledged that Claire and Juria did not have full faith in her yet; she intended to show them why they should.

Her vampire lust and hunger was the potent force that she had to keep in check. So far she had functioned so well in that respect, although both Claire and Juria drove her pulse upward.

As that pulse ascended, Viktoria would leave briefly before that tidal need overwhelmed her.

Already those cravings were gently alighting upon her sex. The delicious beauty of Claire and the handsome hardness of Juria were taking a growing toll upon her.

She threw back at them, "My name is Viktoria."

As she made this motion with her head, her lustrous long dark hair flew separate from her neck and her shoulders. She did this intentionally.

She desired that her amazing assets impacted them. She sought to bond them to her. Heat between the three would serve that purpose so well. She smiled beautifully at the prospect of where their joint passions would take them.

She wrenched her focus back to the search.

Her ability to view the future had been neutralized, it seemed. The mental barrier that she was so unfamiliar with still stalked her brain completely.

Viktoria's frustration was absolute. Her reliance upon signs given her by the forest, Claire and Juria the same, was all that she had. Her only advantage superior to theirs now was her flight. And she would resort to that when an expansive view of the terrain trumped.

She knew that all of their combined resources were required to succeed.

She acutely sensed the power of her foe's arsenal might be equal or greater than hers; perhaps a superhuman arsenal at that.

Chapter 17

Never Far

In the deeper recesses of his now partially tucked away thinking mind, he knew that he was also human.

Yet he presently had an ability to peer easily through the shrouded night, alas without benefit of color of any kind. His hearing was torture some as it was so acute and intense. Odors, on the other hand, were very weak.

In his current incarnation, this all was completely in synch with the wild animal that he was now.

It was only in reflection as the other that these traits of his shocked. Once having born the change, he knew though, that this was as it would always be for him.

He had been there when Viktoria first encountered Claire and Juria.

He had stood poised to strike her down if she had even indicated the subtlest of signals of beginning harm to the couple; Claire in particular.

His senses were keen and attuned. He was invisible to all, even Viktoria, he was so still. His huge bulk merged absolutely into the forested cavern of high rising pine and low lying brush.

His eyes had glittered then and grew large in anticipation of a foul move by the shape shifter. The raising of his hackles was automatic as the fur at neck base and humped shoulders lifted high. Energy was coursing into his paws in anticipation of charging forward; snout pulled back and elevated with snarl at the ready. Under long dark fur, his muscles were tensed so rigidly that the faintest of animal trembling began. His fangs remained pocketed but were immediately accessible when the goal of maiming or killing stormed him. His crouch had the potential for velocity and strength beyond belief.

He was probably an adversary equal to Viktoria.

But nothing triggered a need to attack her then. She had flown in, morphed for just moments, advanced toward the woman and man, then had left abruptly. She took to flight again, wings fanning the sky furiously, receding at breath taking speed.

He was now paralleling their movements just a short distance from them.

Viktoria had returned in beguiling human form and the three were launching their search for Hansel and Gretel through the resisting forest. He kept up with them; soundless and without their recognition of his presence.

He, as Viktoria, also had superhuman qualities. Those qualities would long be in the innocent woman's service. How could she know that he was never far and that his entire mission was her safety?

He didn't know why her safety was his mission; he just felt it and knew that it was. As wolf, he acted, he only thought primitively.

So he simply kept pace with the she-beast, Claire and Juria. His clip matched their clip, stride for stride.

His night vision allowed him to focus on Viktoria's actions even while moving at an explosive pace, as this was. The laggards were Claire and

Juria. Viktoria had to chronically stop so that the couple could catch up with her. They rested briefly then too.

Juria was rarely gasping for breath as Claire was. Her clothes were torn and her fragile skin was scratched and slightly bleeding at her shins where roots, brambles and tiny branches caught at her tender limbs. The wolf was instinctively aware that Claire's exposure from torn clothing and scant bleeding acted as a goad to Viktoria. He was ever watchful, more so as Claire's clothing was shredded and her bleeding increased. He also was instinctively aware that Claire would not cease in the pace set by Viktoria until the children were found.

His wolfish heart pounded at Claire's beauty, grace and goodness under duress. His animal cock stirred too. But he was here to protect Claire and so ignored as best he could his fattening organ. In this manner, he managed to stay semisoft and not let his arousal interfere.

They were all resting. Juria was quietly tending to Claire's tiny wounds by pressing leaves against the worst offending openings. He would kiss her lower legs as he ministered to her. It was meant as comfort for Claire and that is exactly how she took it. She placed her hand on the crown of his head as he kneeled and left it there, toying with his sweaty curls just a tiny bit.

As the wolf paused too, he focused on Viktoria intensively.

She was impatient in manner. She paced in a small circle and glared into the dank forest over and over.

What the wolf pegged his attention to though was not Viktoria's urgent demeanor but in instants where Viktoria would peer at Claire, especially when Claire ripped a ruined piece of clothing from her in frustration and exasperation. It was a minute square of cloth at Claire's bust line. Inadvertently, as Claire pulled on the damnable hanging shred, she ripped more than anticipated and desired. Dream cleavage of hers was now very visible. Mounding upper curve of one breast was there for all to lust over.

He sensed Viktoria's hunger most prominently. Her stare was locked upon Claire. Without control, Viktoria barely touched her own breast. And then she turned away. He knew that her control was ebbing. He did not look away from Viktoria. He could not; not without risking Claire's security.

He searched for signs of the children also as he conformed to the others motion. They had, obviously, had no luck of their own. He had not sensed, seen nor gleaned any clues of his own as to their whereabouts from the separate path that he was taking.

Claire's fears for the children were mysteriously transferred to him as well. And those fears of hers were piercing. Her pain for them escalated with each passing second. The wolf felt the dramatic intensity of her interior pain. It drove him to pursue the hunt for the children equal to her pursuit. And, the longer the children eluded all of them, the greater the likelihood of their suffering or demise.

The threesome pitched forward again. He followed suit. Night was spinning increasingly toward the dawn. This would force direction to shift for all of them. How much longer could they all squeeze out their continued ramble through the wooded tangle?

He did not know the importance of the dawn for them except through intuition. His wolf was excruciatingly sensitive in this manner.

On a very primitive level so much was available to him. It was sublimely intoxicating to have this power and so many other powers also. There was a natural joy, a lovely stretching, experienced inside a body so naturally aware, so massively strong, swift, keen and brutally overwhelming. His presently passive human essence was all that held him back from soaring into his wolf form. And that human essence was soon to regain its sway. The coming day would dictate that.

He knew that his time was short when Viktoria suddenly disappeared in a flap of gigantic black wings and churning air. His skin was beginning to feel its odd sensations.

Chapter 18

Woodsman's Ambivalence

It continued a long trail without results. Claire's exhaustion was setting in. She was laboring over most every step that she took. Shadows were withdrawing fractionally but noticeably. He supposed that Claire was bearing it this well only because of the buzz of her fear for the children, fear of the woods itself, her fear of Victoria. Fear pushed her; she never curled up under fear's onslaught.

She was oozing slivers of blood from her lower legs and had to be cold as more and more of her clothing was parted from her body. Again, he guessed that her anguish over the children's plight was huge because his was so exquisitely excruciating. Their guide was a frightening unknown, a potent enigma.

Juria was both repelled and attracted by Viktoria's beauty, determination and powers. His trepidation regarding her went to the notion of what would make a stranger want to be of such assistance to them. Her transformations earlier utterly spooked him. Was she a rare Good Samaritan or a being come up from hellish depths to torment them more?

He knew that she could have harmed them already had she wanted to. He and Claire were entirely intact to this point, happily.

He was afraid too of dropping his guard within her close proximity. That close proximity to her consistently lured and lulled his senses as if she had invisible threads drawing him and then anesthetizing him into submission. His hesitancy was that she would drain him for her own evil purposes; then Claire would be absolutely on her own against this dark beauty.

He willed himself to maintain all of his bearing on his beloved Hansel and Gretel. That was his means and method not to fall victim to her potency. Riveting his attention upon Claire was another manner in which he could disregard Viktoria's effect upon him.

He was ashamed that Viktoria had any impact upon him at all!

It was crucial now for him to concentrate on the objects of their search. He sensed Hansel and Gretel's great peril. He hated that his skills as a woodsman and hunter had been thwarted throughout the night. It was as if the children had ceased to exist and were beyond all reach. He groaned in his powerlessness and lack of capability.

What did Claire feel? What were Viktoria's true intentions? Uncertainty was leaving him to silently gasp and choke on his own bile and failure. He prayed to God for aid and succor.

It was in that instant, when he flung his wishes heavenward, that Viktoria suddenly ceased to move. She slowly pivoted and threw a paralyzing stare into his eyes. There was the smallest of upward slant at each mouth corner. To him, that eye lock between them sent a single message. The message communicated was of God's absence and of her presence. It was a crushing, draining moment for Juria.

Neither Juria nor Claire was naïve to the fact that Viktoria was a vampire. So, what of the lore of the vampire did Juria have at his disposal as Viktoria faced forward and the three of them trekked in relative uniform cadence. The depth of his knowledge of that grisly lore of hers was quite vast. He had had a fascination with these particular creatures at length. The fascination had been primitive and instinctual; that of craven desire to wonder at magnificent abilities and eternal life.

Actually, both he and Danika had bantered about the subject. Both agreed that if the gift were other than simply fantasy, it would be a beautifully wicked way to live. As Juria, though, learned more and more of the legend, the less he was attracted to the notion. Eventually, he was left with a remnant of appeal but, principally, repulsion toward the evil and human death of it all. Ultimately, he could not fathom the greedy reflex that maintained human sacrifice so that his own being would be endlessly supported!

Finding that the myth was reality and that Viktoria was the only example he had ever encountered of the reality moved beyond his grasp.

His mind was gripped with anaphylaxis and the shock still thundered through him each time that he peered at Viktoria. Her form was so human; how could she be such an unholy, cruel demon rife only with her own need to survive. Yet she wanted his children to escape the wood's nasty snare unscathed. What demon, truly, wanted that?

Juria's store of knowledge was thus: vampires could die. The sun's rays were anathema to a vampire's existence. The body would transform and vanish at the scarcest touch of light's heat and radiance upon them. That would happen with Viktoria?

Harm came from other sources as well, supposedly. A revenant died if staked; staked through the heart with wood from the Hawthorn, Ash or Oak. Death was instantaneous and irrevocable. No trace of the body lingered.

Bullets that were fully silvered served the fatal purpose as well if shot through the heart just under the left nipple. The pulse of the beast beat most dramatically there.

A severed head positioned between the corpse's feet extinguished their spirit perpetually.

A vampire could be made to remain at a distance also. The likes of garlic, wild roses, Christian crosses, turned out mirrors, consecrated ground kept them at bay. Juria remembered all of this in a burst. To know thy enemy most assuredly was to defeat thy enemy. Juria felt well-armed.

Ah though, she was so exquisitely beautiful; and not at all bloated or decomposed in any fashion as he imagined these creatures should be.

In stark reversal of enamored thought, he reached around to clasp Claire's ivory hand behind him. It took but an instant for Claire to unlock their intertwined fingers to gasp and point at a white patch of wool fabric hooked upon a tiny low lying branch which Claire recognized as cloth torn from one of Hansel or Gretel's sleeves. At last, a sign of the children's presence earlier.

Claire was trembling. Juria put an arm out to hold Claire back from sweeping into the area. One sign might lead to others nearby. That was Juria's hope, at least. Viktoria halted also and smiled. My god, such a warm smile too Juria noted. He scanned the area methodically. Visually, he picked a square portion of ground framing the fabric. Even if he found nothing else, this discovery was welcome beyond belief.

Sound and wind suddenly swirled around Claire and Juria. He could hear the flap of wings. He maintained his stare on the white material. The rest was superfluous. And, besides, he knew it was Viktoria morphing forms and sprinting away on currents of air. Heat of the almost sunrise was impossible to ignore after the frigidity of the night.

Juria felt the excitement of possible search success.

Claire placed her hands on his broad shoulders as he bent over and seared the ground with his seeking gaze. Claire rubbed his shoulders lightly and unconsciously. Strangely, his relaxation there heightened his concentration. With the oncoming sun, his eyes were drawn to the surface highlighted by her flickering elbow shadows. That was how he discovered a further clue. It was the merest indentation of where a portion of a child's largest bare toe had trod. The incomplete print partially protruded from under a leaf; a partial of a partial in a sector of moist soil. It pointed forward and told Juria that hope remained and hope lay directly ahead.

Every trace of them bolstered his hopes for the children's survival.

Chapter 19

Thoughts Awry

Her nipples were turgid and tingling at all times. Her bodice had been rent open some so that the frosting atmosphere had heavy effect upon her skin. She longed for a release from the sensation somehow. But there was not a means while they tracked Hansel and Gretel.

Her calves were scratched unmercifully also. Between the ache of her lower body, the shrill and pleasurable feeling of her upper body, her fatigue and anxiety, even with Juria's close proximity and support, she was in a much weakened state.

She and Juria had not eaten at length and she was ravenous. Her children came before all else though. And she drove herself to keep pace with Juria and Viktoria. She refused to be the reason for any slowdown in their hunt.

But her thoughts were scattered and wildly awry; so beyond her control. She squeezed her eyes shut quickly whenever she needed and tossed her head determinedly to attempt to break the thoughts away and force them elsewhere.

Claire's barriers were crumbling.

She had no capacity to manage those reflections anymore. All she could manage now was to press on and keep up.

The most unsettling images targeted Viktoria. These added to the erotic sensation that the cold hand of the air had already initiated upon her nipples. She hated it when her loins began to lubricate in spite of all efforts otherwise; that entire region of hers simmered in a broth of unwanted desire. Her attempts at erotic discipline only seemed to create the fuel that ignited this passion.

She capitulated and let her attention drift as she recognized fruitless effort for what it was.

One fantasy in particular was confoundingly delicious. She floated there helplessly. She was branded by Viktoria's face; a face that drew her to it unreservedly. She marveled at the smooth and flawless skin of that face, the angular majesty of those cheekbones, the magnetic fullness of her lips. Claire imagined putting her hand to that face and letting her fingers linger. That fancy created a buzz within her; an excitement immediately transferred to breast, belly, opening and the crimson button at tiny throne above her opening.

Claire was modest but never had any false allusions about her figure. It was a figure she was proud of. She never flaunted that build and she never hid it either. The physical facet that she most cherished was that of her finely sculpted petite bottom.

Second to that though, she was pleased by the size of her breasts. They flared starkly from her lean frame. The square bodice of her apron less dirndl held her breasts in place; yet Claire could not move impulsively without risk that her very large mounds would fly from the material. She was not given to sudden motion as she constantly paid attention to this fact.

The plentiful quality of her bosom was roundly surpassed by Viktoria's. Claire was stunned at how much larger Viktoria's breasts were than her own.

The diaphanous folds of Viktoria's garment had hid almost nothing, the dark night more effective at this than the clothing. Viktoria's outline was magnificent. Her ebony globes hung from her chest perfectly.

They were full and pendulous with the barest of swing and sway, black areolas large and occasionally crinkled, nipples long and thick even before arousal ensued.

In Claire's mind's eye, Claire dropped her fingers to a nipple, stroked it, strummed it and then bent down to it. She registered its soft and elastic feel, its definite heat, felt its surge as she lashed her tongue back and forth over Viktoria's tip. Viktoria cupped her breasts and held them out to Claire slowly, almost casually.

The dark woman was standing, had spread her legs wide apart and angled her head backwards; eyes closed and breathing hushed in anticipation. Claire wandered lower, kissing flat expanse of warm belly to demarcation between body and one thigh, then the other thigh. Viktoria sucked on one of her own nipples as she spread her legs ever wider, sex at Claire's disposal.

Claire descended, separated Viktoria's lips, licked at the gleam between. She dipped her tongue into the beckoning orifice; swirling it inside. The first sounds escaped Viktoria's mouth. It was a quiet continuous moan. She pushed Claire's head deeper into her hot cleft, her legs vibrated faintly. She also squatted just barely; all the better to have tighter contact, greater pleasure.

Juria clasped Claire's fingers. She was jolted back to reality and simultaneously spotted a tag of white flannel cloth.

She pointed, certain it was a sleeve fragment from Gretel's sleepwear. They were not rescued yet but this was a beginning . . . . finally.

She tensed to rush to it. Juria's arm restrained her. Yes, she must not disturb the surroundings. Her anguish would be overwhelming if she trampled the area and destroyed further clues in the process. "Thank You, Juria" she whispered.

Juria was already engrossed in his examination and did not respond to her whisper.

A whoosh behind her startled her severely. She spun around in time to observe the moments ago beautiful Viktoria reconfigure herself into that terrifyingly ugly and receding winged form.

Claire was suddenly skeptical about her return. Had she abandoned them? A bursting sadness passed through her. She returned her energies to Juria. Damn the sadness! She would have it be gone.

And it was; dissipating as violently as it had come. Juria and the children required her assistance, her unvarnished attention. Hands lightly went to Juria's shoulders. It was an automatic and supportive gesture of hers whenever connection had to be reestablished.

Juria swept a leaf away and was transfixed; transfixed and then ecstatic. Claire was unable to visualize anything at all. There it was suddenly, a child's toe print. Under his breath, Juria whispered to the forest floor, "We are correct. Yes, their direction is as we travel."

He swiveled his head toward her and blew out a breath in relief. "It is Gretel. They have passed this way. The print points ahead, to the west. No further blind guessing for us. They are here, they are alive and that is so sweet!"

Claire joined in his joy and celebration. Tiny kisses fell from her mouth onto his shoulders and neck. She could hardly stop. She clasped him hard from behind. Then she released her grasp on him and twirled happily, forgetting to be careful. They were both so glad!

Then she sat heavily, worn and weary. "Juria, I am feeling dizzy and faint. We cannot slow the pace but I have to eat something, anything my love. How can we do both?"

And Claire began to cry, to sob without control. What would become of Hansel and Gretel if either Juria or Claire faltered now?

It was horrible to consider failure just when it felt as if they were on the verge of rendering positive this hideous time. She was not able to stand it. She could not, would not, consider failure in any way, shape or form for any reason whatsoever!

Chapter 20

Enduring Pact

There was an all engulfing sudden absence of function. His brain wavered, shuttered and closed with a vicious slam. This was when he lost every shred of cognition, any remnant of consciousness and awareness as either a wolf or a human being. He could not know what contortions his body, mind and spirit experienced for the next two minutes.

The change was violent and perfectly consuming. Furious amounts of energy were spent in the transformation. Any who had the misfortune to see the metamorphosis would cringe in terror. He always fell instantly, injury or no; though any injury from the fall was fixed with the changes that occurred. His vulnerability after the fall was profound as was his apparent helplessness to all. He was never warned beforehand by an aura of any kind. The collapse was total and unstoppable.

Tremors poured through his arms and legs, his neck stiffened and then spasmed wickedly. His eyes fluttered and then blinked continuously while his eyeballs rolled up and under those half closed eyelids. The writhing of the body would begin then. Shedding of fur occurred in a tsunami of wavelike motion. Bones splintered and snapped in the sound of a bonfire sparking the wood within its flames. Skin stretched and tore and then reformed.

He became a seething mass of transfiguration. His snout sucked itself in and his ears wilted, flattened and rounded; claws to toes, tail to buttocks also ensued. It was the ugliest of physical symphonies one could observe or experience. Yet it was equally magnificent in the breadth of change wrought upon his body; it was unimaginable, wolf to man or man to wolf.

He stood up and felt the usual slight soreness in his every joint. His thoughts were syrupy and slow. That too was familiar each and every occurrence. He put his palm to his face and felt the hairless skin of nose, cheeks, and chin. He inhaled deeply. And experienced the chill of the vanishing night; yet the warmth of the newly rising sun counteracted the chill.

His nudity always surprised him each and every time as it made him feel vastly exposed and irritatingly disposed to take time away from Claire to redress himself. This meant at least an hour away in order to find his nearest self-made deposit of clothes dropped and hidden in knapsacks speckled throughout the woods. So now he fled to those clothes.

This time was different though. In spite of his clothes needing to be obtained as rapidly as possible, he paused to peer down at his nudity. Was it the sight of both Viktoria and Claire together that made him erect and huge in this moment? And he could not ignore his cock's call either. It had to have been that the two ravishing women viewed in unison had had a pronounced effect upon him.

The eroticism of the trek of the ebony and ivory beauties paralyzed him. He had to briefly hide and find a way to release himself. Or why hide; that would just add excess time to an episode that should not even be happening at all. His tall erection, thick tube, and clear dew drop at rounded end seized his spirit exclusively.

He sat abruptly upon the ground, fisted and stroked his organ deliciously. As his thoughts curled around the lush forms of the women, he could not resist the urgent call of his now thicker massive member and pumped his encircled hand over it tightly. He flashed a thumb over one of his nipples as well. This multiplied the deep sensation tenfold or more easily. As a matter of fact, he could not pour himself out without including his nipples from beginning to end. He had realized the sensitivity of them equal to the sensitivity of a woman's nipples long ago and indulged in the action without guilt. As he initiated his nipple touch, his cock swelled further as he pounded upon it with all of nature watching.

His exposure became increasingly sensual as time elapsed and he fell further under the spell of his self desire. He was aware that he had to be quick and, by sheer force of his fantasies, would be uncontrolled as well.

Viktoria played upon his mind first. She was a wealth of perfect features; possibly too perfect. His intake of air caught in his throat as he pictured her sensual face, her impossibly high and outsized breasts topped with long and full dark nipples. They must be so sensitive and tender to ministrations of fingers, lips. What would her moans sound like? Would she beg for more using his name?

He threw his head back then, closed his eyes, and slowed his rhythm; he wanted to take his cock gently for a second. Alternating with the potent strokes, he took his cockhead only with circled thumb and forefinger only, rubbing his crown gently up and down, over and over. The alternating rhythm of strong with gentle was delightful and rich in sensation.

He wanted to taste Viktoria too. Taste her heat, moisture, and pulse at her epicenter.

Then Viktoria's image receded somewhat and an ivory goddess swept in. Claire was equally gorgeous with Viktoria. He had been affected increasingly by her as the material of her bodice had been torn away, fragment by fragment. He had caught swing and sway shadows of platter size golden brown areolas and largely pointed nipples upon her high yet wonderfully pendulous bulging breasts.

His thoughts were seized as one, than the other, woman overtook his passion, switching more and more swiftly as he varied his stroke, gentle to strong with intense acceleration.

Briefly, the Guardian, who was distantly related to Claire, allowed his mind to alight on the disappointment that Henry would have showered upon him, rebuking him for his present behavior. Once the Guardian had become a werewolf, something that he had never sought, he was crushed emotionally when he reflected upon it while in human form. Claire had bound herself to an individual whom Henry felt was inferior. At this point, Henry bound him to a pact enduring. Her father had been so generous while the Guardian struggled to emerge from a troubled youth that the Guardian was compelled to pay the man back. When the Guardian's powers were sadly acquired, he told Henry of his newfound capabilities. Claire's father saw the advantage in those powers and demanded that the Guardian comply in protecting his precious daughter. It was an action that the Guardian complied with immediately. Claire had no choice in the decision. This was a decision between the two men. And he meant to keep it!

Yet, how was he protecting Claire now? He wasn't!

He could not stop himself however. And he did not cease as his organ deepened, lengthened, reddened, enslaved him and his hands. All organized thought vanished as he came closer to releasing himself. His throb obliterated him. He spread his legs widely to enhance all sensation. His large scrotum twitched slightly and constricted minutely. His threshold, his one arm pumping furiously and the other thumb flicking insistently, was being sought and was imminent. It was then that he breached that exquisite threshold.

He had abandoned the gentle stroke and was mercilessly stroking himself. Suddenly he was riven with feeling so powerful that he had no alternative but to yield to it. There was a tiny pause where he went rigid, and then he squeezed his cock and held it. He gasped then and quick eruptions of pearly streams shot fiercely from his bulging crimson cockhead. Many veins were clear and pulsing at the sides of his jerking soft club. A dozen spraying strands flew to the forest surface.

With remnants of come still upon his cock, he now fled to his clothes.

Chapter 21

Find Her

Juria was ecstatic. He still had his forest prowess. Even as he took long strides through the panoply of trees and their webbed entanglements, he spotted nuances and signs that led both Claire and him to an inviting entry. He laughed silently as he knew that any door would be enticing at this point of their seemingly endless and fruitless slog. He was uncertain as to the owner but both he and Claire's hopes flared at the possibility that it might be Viktoria's home.

Both had whispered to one another that Viktoria was so capable that any successful search required her intensely focused presence. Besides that, she could fly and scan huge swaths of ground in condensed intervals.

Midpoint in the day, Juria had seen the faintest outline of a shoe print; a shoe print larger than what Hansel or Gretel possessed. Even though evidence told Viktoria that the children had been snatched, this print confirmed to Juria that the children were not alone. And was it conceivably a feminine imprint? It was not, no, as no woman was of capacity to outwit them all this way he surmised. So, there was at least one other leading the children. Juria concluded that they were neither lost nor unprotected. He and Claire felt relief that this was so, as now they did not have to forge ahead as intensively fearing the children's immediate demise; Hansel and Gretel would not be ravaged unmercifully by the forest.

Yet they still had to pursue quickly as they had no idea of Hansel and Gretel's safety with an unknown, powerful and likely dangerous stranger.

Juria could not grasp any of this. He was as if blind and stumbling without likelihood of touching a familiar object. Nothing anchored him; everything eluded him. Claire, though she cherished them, did not have the intuition of a mother, simply as a stepmother. Though that was mighty, it was not blood. The urgency of love and faith were all he had in this moment. He filled his lungs with air, turned the doorknob and prayed that love and faith would suffice.

He also chose to protect Claire at all costs in their seeking. He was adamant with himself that no member of his family would come to ultimate harm. So he waved Claire off slightly as he entered the darkening place. Shadows were deepening as the heavy sun began chasing its path below the horizon. It seemed inconceivable that daylight was already peeling away into night.

Juria scanned those interior shadows and visualized nothing awry at first glance. Quiet dominated the fore space of what must have been the primary room. Then he saw it, the exploded and mangled door Viktoria had spoken of to them. It was Viktoria's cottage.

But why had the main door been unlocked for any and all to enter? She must have been in a massive rush! Shifting his thoughts back and forth, he let his gaze drift to the splintered wood to his right. What remained of it was lit by occasional darts of sun with fragile dust moats lazily rising within those shafts of yellow. The crushed door had not been moved for a length of time, if at all.

There was the palest scent of earth that worked on his nose, his brain; gently moist it was. Juria glanced Claire's way as if to say, "Follow, but cautiously."

Claire softly stepped forward, leaned in toward Juria and then paused as he paused. Her dance matched his dance at all moments here in this eerie shelter at twilight; he sensed her fright. Together they stepped fully inside.

That nearly nonexistent pungent scent of earth directed his footsteps. The odor was both attractive and repellant simultaneously as it lingered and mixed with his breathing. It grew in strength as he slowly made his way to what was a tiny kitchen; neat and spotless yet totally utilitarian as if no comfort was found in food here.

There was a downward slanting stairwell then, if one even chose to call it that, barely exposed at one corner. The odor became dank and musty as they approached; it was no longer faint or particularly pleasant. Had the children, when here, detected this smell or had they been too exhausted to have noticed? Juria contemplated that thought for the briefest of seconds.

Claire proceeded behind him as well with eyes wide and palm of one hand gently laid over her mouth and nose. He touched her trembling body. A chill, silent air began to surround them. The steps were so very narrow and really nothing more than slats to give one direction and balance. Handrails were not in existence here. Juria stopped after the third slat so that his eyes could adjust to the thickly pervading, unyielding black gloom.

After a frozen minute, Juria saw what he expected. It was the outline of a finely tooled burial box. They had found Viktoria. He and Claire were totally aware of what she was. They no longer cringed. His fear was smashed in the wave of their need for Viktoria's assistance. And she seemed so willing to give just that to them.

She drew him to her besides; Claire too. So consternation was now put aside for the greater good of the children. "Please God, have Viktoria truly be with us," was Juria's greatest wish and a great test of faith for him.

The lid was tightly sealed. Nothing would pass through it. Viktoria was utterly protected in her beautiful high gloss tomb. Juria and Claire finished the last several slats and stepped away from the coffin, leaned against the dugout soil wall and waited. The setting sun would bring a rising Viktoria.

Clack, clack pierced the now pitch black space. Juria had been clasping Claire tightly to give her warmth, comfort, strength but the sudden staccato sound made him hug her so tightly. She shrank into his powerful arms. They both stared in horrible fascination at what might emerge from the sarcophagus.

He was stunned, as he imagined Claire was also, when Viktoria's dark silhouette pushed up from her container. She was neither deformed nor in other than human appearance; she was clothed, beautiful. He had anticipated the worst, hardly this. Viktoria smiled graciously at them.

"Ah, you tracked my whereabouts so well. I am proud of you. Was the unlocked front door a surprise? It was intentional. And I was in the rush of the damned."

Her smile widened so that her teeth gleamed. Viktoria threw her head back at this and gave a full throated laugh. Juria was beginning to guess that Viktoria was not completely satisfied with her undead status. He sensed her ambivalence and further guessed that an ironic sense of humor must have eased her uncertainty and confusion. His instincts had always been a razor sharp guide of his and had rarely been a hindrance.

Viktoria went on to say, "I also can sometimes see forward into the future. I was well aware you would be present as I awoke."

Again the wryness broke out in her words. "Unfortunately, this seems not to be with the children. Even omniscience seems to have its unkind limitations."

"I must leave you again though as I am famished. So please excuse me for a short while."

Viktoria bounded out of her confines and flew up the stairwell, transfiguring herself as she went. Juria had witnessed this shape shifting already but remained transfixed in its power and hideousness. He emotionally contracted to think of her in her bat form.

Claire gasped deeply at this sight. They were equally astounded and horrified. To Juria, this was an almighty power unleashed. Woe to any in that power's path.

The mass of solid air was whipped by her winged motion. He was, however, strangely comforted by knowing that she would return and the search would begin again in earnest.

Juria grasped Claire's hand and whispered, "We will trust her. She will be back to aid us. Let us renew our hunt again."

Chapter 22

Parent's Blindness

Adelaide fretted so. She was very concerned about her Henry. He paced throughout so many of his waking hours; or rocked incessantly in his favorite chair. The furrows that were etching themselves horizontally across his forehead and vertically between his brows were of the recent sort; as recent as Claire and Juria's engagement. Henry had only relented regarding the wedding because he, and she herself, could not deny their daughter anything, for better or worse. But this nearly destroyed him and her some.

He still steamed and stewed over images of his golden daughter with that unrefined man! Oh how Henry loathed Juria.

He had told Adelaide that many times over. Henry impressed upon Adelaide his view that Juria was coarse, uncultured, stupid and even insensitive. Though Adelaide had an altogether separate sense of Juria, she loved Henry and stood with him, never against him.

She was certain that Juria was passionately, almost obsessively, connected to their Claire. For that quality alone, Adelaide appreciated Juria. Yet it was very curious as Claire had had vast numbers of high quality suitors pursue her avidly. So why had she picked Juria? Adelaide was perplexed at that. And she was doubly perplexed that her very reasonable daughter, her beautiful child, had been single-mindedly insistent upon a union with Juria. There had been no dissuading Claire. Henry had been the furious bull and Adelaide had been the gentle lamb. Nothing, though, had deterred Claire from having the woodcutter.

So what now, Adelaide wondered? Her only child, her greatest creative gift to this often strange and careless world, was in apparent disarray concerning her choice of lifelong partner. Claire was neither a rebellious child, nor a rebellious, irresponsible adult either. Adelaide took heart in that that was true of her always precocious and exquisitely unique daughter. To Adelaide, her child spilled bright light in that she had so many capabilities. Adelaide treasured Claire's uninhibited forthrightness for one; laced with diplomacy of delivery such that others never felt any lash from her tongue. Ah, and Claire had an automatic willingness to provide support, love and empathy to those in genuine need of succor. Claire was fervent about offering all that she had to lift another up; she never asked for anything in return. Her charm and grace were equally luminescent. She attracted one and all it seemed.

This Mother, Adelaide, was biased as any mother would be toward their cherished offspring. Adelaide waxed silently eloquent regarding Claire but did not drown in giddy waves of overestimation. Claire's fundamental beauty of being went past all lack of objectivity so that even a mother was aware of the true reality of one so special.

Then, again, why Claire's determined allegiance to Juria? Adelaide continued to agonize on this seeming inconsistency in her daughter. It confused Adelaide, incensed Henry, and perplexed their friends and those occasional acquaintances that they confided in. Adelaide must have overlooked qualities in the woodcutter beyond the obvious.

Even though Henry dismissed even the obvious in Claire's husband, Adelaide did not. She attempted to give the man his due, somewhat.

Also, she preferred to grant their daughter her ability to size up a man well and then steadfastly link herself permanently to that man. Yes, Juria had great physical presence and prowess, was handsome in a blunt kind of way, could track well and cut timber well, provided-only to a degree in her mind-for Claire and her Step grandchildren's needs. There had to be more, much more to Juria than just this though to maintain Claire's ardor for him. The difference between Henry and Adelaide's feeling's on this grossly raw subject was that Adelaide yielded to the idea of positive potential and possibilities within Juria. She had to trust that Claire's judgment in the man somehow had to cut a logical picture; so she gave their marriage the benefit of the doubt as often as she was able. But it tasted so bitter in her mouth.

Not so Henry! He was of the fiery opinion that his daughter was wonderfully sane on all issues except for her inexplicable love for Juria. Henry, she understood to her core, was determined to save his brilliant and beautiful daughter from her only insane life decision. He would have it no other way. He was deeply blinded to there even being a smidgeon of redemption for Juria. Henry would rather slash himself before yielding to Juria as good or good for Claire. Never!

Adelaide quaked at the fury roiling inside of Henry. She prayed that they survived this fractured time in their lives.

Their doorknocker broke the tense silence in the household. Adelaide gasped, shivered and crossed her hand over to her heart. Her bosom heaved in alarm. She was shocked and stunned as well. It was late and they seldom had visitors at night. She and Henry should have been in bed themselves at this hour.

Henry burst from his rocker and shoved at Adelaide to stand aside. An unannounced visit was unwanted, unwarranted and even had potentially dangerous implications. No matter the suddenness, the uncommon roughness, he would not have his wife risk harm. Adelaide forgave the sharpness from him as she was fully cognizant of his utter protectiveness of her and of Claire when she too resided here.

Henry marched to the door and unbolted the lock so that a gun's retort seemed to have rung out. He stood at the door's opening as he barely moved the edge from the frame. Adelaide was paralyzed. She knew not what to expect and was terrified as she observed no flicker or flame of torchlight falling on the walls of their inner chamber.

From Henry came a cry; several cries echoed back. Adelaide rushed to him as he opened the door with a vengeance; and then a happy chortle that stupefied Adelaide. She reached the entry in only a few swift strides now, heart thumping strongly against her vibrating ribcage.

She raced to Henry as he lurched outside as if totally drunk. Hansel and Gretel joyfully swarmed Henry's bending form. They squealed and wiggled wildly in his grasp, tears nearly bursting out as he enfolded them in his pipe sized arms. He nuzzled them and they kissed him back. Adelaide was at everyone's side quickest as she tossed her arms around them all. It had been so long since Hansel and Gretel had come and seen their Stepmother's parents.

They relished and loved one another . . . . obviously. The children were especially delighted this time as they were also ready to come in from a long journey outdoors.

Adelaide glanced upward and then quizzically scrutinized Hansel. "Where are your parents?"

He paused and then sobbed once, twice. He could not get any words out.

"Right here." Adelaide and her husband simultaneously jerked their heads toward the voice. They glimpsed a dark figure in the even darker night black. That figure approached.

Chapter 23

Bad Moon Rising

What the Guardian observed during this phase of the search was to cause him to reel and pull back and forth in intense uncertain emotion. The actions of Juria, Claire and Viktoria would become so unpredictable that he would not know how to proceed. So he proceeded strictly and was on highest alert to ensure Claire's wellbeing.

The events unraveled quite slowly, though at the first indication of inconsistencies in word and or behavior, the Guardian was wolfishly tense and acutely prepared to insert himself rapidly if Claire became at risk for any reason.

Earlier, in human guise and fully clothed, he had witnessed Claire and Juria as they struggled forward on a path of faint and difficult to discover and then discern clues.

The Guardian did not hear their words while in man form as his aural senses became dull, mercilessly dull, then. He guessed at their progress solely via their actions. He did not miss many words anyhow as Juria and Claire automatically operated in synchronization with one another quietly. Love had potent qualities to be sure.

He had wandered into questions while in human incarnation which were not always pertinent but were a simple matter of curiosity. Had the married pair come upon the cottage strictly by coincidence or were they seeking the she demon out?

And what persuaded them to do that if true? Did they think her an ally and friend? That would be an unholy alliance; yet would that be anymore peculiar than being protected by a wolf man? Life itself was thoroughly peculiar anyhow what with contradictions, ironies and inconsistency's triumphing more often than not.

So he was left with the possibility that Juria and Claire had befriended Viktoria in the midst of their plight. Unusual circumstances bred unusual bedfellows seemed to be an apt phrase in this case. But how far taken and to what limits applied? These unknowns were about to be revealed according to his impressions of their spontaneous and voluptuous entwining.

Juria and Claire had exited the cottage with Viktoria at their side momentarily. Then she had rippled into primitive shape and had vanished skyward.

The couple barely flinched at this and after only a few seconds pitched themselves back into the shadows, little knowing that close by, a man was clawing his way back to haired and huge beast. The descent of the sun impacted him as powerfully as it impacted Viktoria; though light of day was not lethal for him whatsoever.

He moved on all fours to follow now but could rise and walk on two legs anytime.

His creature instincts resonated with the crude sense that Viktoria's return was imminent; unsightly blood removed, uncontrolled hunger dampened, she joined them as they trudged ahead.

His hearing was expanded and he heard their every word; animal relief at the fact that guesswork for him had diminished. He served her with much more confidence.

Claire's appearance persisted in having devastating effect upon his organ, be it animal or man. He was outsize and sensitive in that region regardless.

It's very pink and quickly reddening tip slid slightly out from his wolf's sheath. It was stirred by so much of her tattered bodice magnificently bobbling virtually unsecured heavy breasts.

Actually, Claire had to reposition her mounds repeatedly as she surged forward with Juria and Viktoria. As a matter of fact, one oddity in Claire's behavior was when, occasionally in the repositioning, he caught Claire fleetingly flicking a free nipple with her thumb while she stared at Viktoria's posterior outline. The Guardian was perplexed and captivated simultaneously by those very stimulating actions of hers, especially with her nipples lengthening and tightening.

It was definitely not Juria whom she gazed at in these surreptitious moments. Even his wolf self gleaned that her fascination was with Viktoria's sumptuous rear.

His animal eyes took Viktoria in in almost a predatory manner because he was so smitten with her beauty as well.

Still, how might Juria have reacted had he been knowledgeable of these subtleties occurring instead of firmly fixing on a successful outcome for the search?

This all might bode a bad moon rising; no immediate telling on that certainly.

The challenge for the Guardian swirled around his expanding cock. He had stretched in length and widened voluminously. The weight was becoming ponderous.

His gait was impeded in equal measure between his cock shifting position awkwardly and the mounting sensation that distracted him severely. Pace was extraordinarily problematic to attain and then maintain with a mountain of straining flesh at his underside.

He noted Viktoria, Juria and Claire stopped abruptly. The Guardian halted as well. His organ was so inflamed and massive; a thick, insistent pulse beat through to his dripping, swollen cockhead. Not only was he thankful at their abrupt halt, his excitement meant that they gave all indications of engaging lustily between themselves.

He heard plenty; he felt more.

Juria's head snapped upward at Viktoria's cessation.

Claire and Viktoria immediately sandwiched Juria and his brow furrowed in brief startle. That look lingered nary an instant the Guardian could not help but notice. Juria's brow softened and relaxed as Viktoria raised her lips, teeth shining, to his. He was immobile and so very taut from head to toe. No blood of his was wasted on unnecessary movement as it coursed to his ever building and surging manhood.

Claire reached to his shirt and without restraint ripped it open. She pinched his nipples in a fashion the wolf was fully aware that he most certainly desired without reserve. Once touched there, he must be helpless as the werewolf's man-side was. She pinched his nipples, one, the other, then again.

She had to relish the firming feel of apparent dramatic effect that it engendered in him.

Viktoria maintained her definite pressure on his parting lips and yet also reached around Juria to gently rub heat into Claire's tight nipples. Then Viktoria shredded the remains of the scant ragged bodice and brought Claire's now gently heaving breasts into full visibility.

Juria dropped a hand down to Viktoria's wet slit.

The Guardian understood that Viktoria's powerful lure had finally overcome Claire who then subdued Juria and teased him into thoroughly participating.

He reminded himself again and again of his promise to Henry and his responsibility to Claire.

Chapter 24

Dissipated Heat

Viktoria charged along, conscious that her allure was provoking Claire into an alien act over which no restraint existed. That was the bewitching influence of the vampire on another's sexual sensibility.

Viktoria's searing craving for them both was about to erupt outward. It was a gnawing, glittering need to swoon in their arms and partake of the chalice of liquid yearning which would indeed gush between them.

Even rescue of the children was being buried briefly by her urge, the ungodly throb that coursed into her vampire center. Sensing that Claire was taking in her every move, Viktoria turned when she could not bear the lusting torment any longer. She was panting, not from exertion, but exclusively from her erotic universe.

When she spun around she faced Juria and this maneuver of hers took him by complete surprise. This caused his head to tilt up and the momentum pushed their lips together. Viktoria's prescience told her that he had fantasized this type of happening, sealing passion with a kiss, but had forced himself not to. He was profoundly in love with Claire and demanded his thick desire for Viktoria go forever underground. With these images, she saw how he fought it so but her foresight foretold that he had to surrender to her.

She was ecstatic that his lips melted into hers as hers melted into his. He let his hand fall to her wet cleft and he explored there.

That Claire would reach for his upper garment from behind him and separate it in two in one violent jerk was known in advance of its happening as well.

Clairvoyance was not nearly enough; she had to immerse herself in the reality instantly and completely. And this was not pursuit of blood or sustenance; it was purely pursuit of connection.

In addition, that Claire was overcome was all part of her plan of seduction. So she also reached around Juria and discovered Claire's nipples with her seeking fingers. The plan was working to a perfection that was becoming so complete that Viktoria allowed herself to succumb to it absolutely. She was in the tempest of body fundaments and emotional need easily equaling the other's needs.

That Viktoria permitted another master to dictate to her here was exceptional. She, Juria and Claire were all now Mother Nature's toys. Their actions became wild and there was no avenue of retreat from their cravings. All hail the God of Impulse and the requisite submission to its energy, Viktoria cheered!

Paying the price of having indulged would come later. Viktoria did not care price presently nor did the other two either. This was too pleasurable to deny. And so she pushed against Juria's seeking fingers, kissed him compulsively and taunted Claire's nipples into a beguiling length that triggered the faintest of moans from the other woman.

As Viktoria incited them, her ardor elevated quickly. Her own nipples had to be placated soon. Her silken top was easy to tear and, as her lips clung to his, tear she did. Her breasts fell and she removed one hand from Claire, cupped one of her own, broke lips from Juria and lifted one of her ebony mounds and midnight tip into his sightline. At this proffering of herself, Viktoria was assured of what he would do next. And he did. Like a new born babe, he suckled her and flicked his tongue over her nipple as he sucked. Her nipple flared and darkened in his mouth, she knew.

She watched also as Claire's fingers continued to pinch and caress his nipples on his broad chest. His pectorals were well defined and lightly covered with the finest of blond filaments that divided his chest symmetrically. He also had the most delicate line of duskier hair emerging from his waistband. This sight caused Viktoria's pulse to intensify.

She was pooling warm slick liquid over his intimately stroking fingers. She spread her legs for him to go deeper into her beautiful cleft.

It was in this moment that Claire dreamily stepped back from Juria and placed herself behind Viktoria. Claire's breath was gentle but heated on Viktoria's neck even with the crisp temperatures surrounding them in their wooded playground. They all blew cold white visible air from their mouths with each exhalation.

Hansel and Gretel would be saved but this had to come first. Viktoria's impulses surged and would not crest soon. She rendered the pair her wanton, irresponsible, hedonistic slaves.

Claire deigned to brush Viktoria's full mane to one side and lavished the faintest of kisses just above her shoulders. Claire moaned into her ear.

The on fire vampire trembled as both Juria and Claire cradled her back and laid her smoothly onto the soft damp grass. Viktoria was oblivious to any hard or irregular object beneath her. She simply had to share herself with them. She opened her eyelids and observed Juria and Claire exchange a puzzled peek between them. It was their wonderment and brief confusion at moving forward into this passion state with a virtual stranger of sympathies not completely recognized. Viktoria discerned this. She branded their glance as their compact with one another that their acquiescence put none of their shared feelings at risk. "How could they really tell?" echoed throughout Viktoria's mind.

Regardless, from that one silent exchange, from that moment on, they allowed themselves to revel in a maelstrom of emotion.

The bodies of Juria and Claire loomed above her. One kneeled at her right side, the other at her left side. Each feasted on one vastly massed breast. To be prostrate and acted upon was rare; no, it did not happen ever. As vampire, Viktoria led without exception until tonight. She delighted in this passivity; all the better to see the extent of the pair's longing for her. She had to witness the extent of that attraction which was now vividly presenting itself to her.

Juria gobbled at her tip, panted and kneaded her fullness. Claire did not touch Viktoria's breast other than with her tongue and lips. Her tongue barely moistened the offered flesh from an underside start narrowing concentrically until she arrived at the hot black point and then suddenly lashed at the firming bud of flesh with outstretched tongue crazy in movement.

Viktoria was never helpless but came closest when either her nipples or lower nub were stimulated. Both taken in union caused the profoundest of release for her. Juria's immediate attack resounded within her while Claire's slow rhythm, and then sudden onslaught consumed her and caused her to writhe and moan beneath their dual ministrations.

Claire flowed deliberately down to Viktoria's clit, dragging her scorching, elongated and ultra-responsive nipples over belly skin as she went.

Viktoria was rapt with need and could not stay still or hush herself.

Juria untied his trouser fall and his loaded organ sprang from the leather confines. He stroked it several times rapidly and it grew wide and long under his hand. Then he squeezed it hard and held it tightly as it reddened and thickened more so immediately. His doing this made Viktoria gasp. Her eyes fastened on the clear and glistening drop which hung delicately from his cockhead's opening.

She took his sizeable manhood in her open mouth as he thrust it into the enveloping o of her lips. She tasted his dew drop and shuddered drunkenly. He held still as she swallowed him over and over. She touched her burning nipples as well.

Claire had already forced Viktoria's legs really wide and moved avidly on Viktoria's tiny epicenter of sensation. Claire thrust two fingers in and out of Viktoria.

Juria swelled enormously in her mouth. He cried out and ejected bursts of come down her throat. She drained him gladly as she snapped waves and contractions into Claire's mouth.

Juria swung his head toward the grass in ecstatic exhaustion. Claire bore down on him in spite of this though and rolled him supine. She then straddled his face. He lapped at her and twisted her heaven sent nipples hard until Claire nearly smothered him in a groaning and magnificent orgasm of her own.

They all three tumbled into a single mass of tangled limbs and dissipated heat.

Chapter 25

More Than Mystified

She peered down at herself aghast. The trance held her ethical self fully immobilized and she was therefore unable to stop the twisting, churning body below her, her own. Her well-balanced self was imprisoned by some spell and her unrestrained self-ruled; ruled such that her body was stimulated by the passionate call of both Juria and Viktoria.

Claire had no alternative but to succumb to the pleasure, the mindless sensations stampeding through her sexual centers. She did not deny that it was heady and delicious to allow herself such freedom in ways not sought or expected before this instant in time.

She had thoroughly believed in her utter conventionality, especially in the matter of sexual involvement. This was beyond her ken. She was more than mystified, yet because of her lack of anticipation or preparedness for this awakening, she was roused to an even larger degree.

She glanced Juria's way, flashed a look of reassurance, as he seemed to back, and forward she dove, hot and ready for whatever delight would now caress her here.

This was for better or worse; one of those huge plunges taken without an inkling of knowledge regarding the outcome. She was risking all yet chasing God's fine hand in her actions as well. Or so she hoped and intuited. Leanly put, God help her!

The three of them sailed through what turned out to be epic for all of them.

When accomplished though, Claire was fully sated and told herself adamantly, once and enough.

She had to communicate that to Viktoria first so that Viktoria's evolved human remnant would dictate and Viktoria would not place vampirish spells on her and Juria anymore.

To Claire, this was a test of the vampire's sincerity, gambling on Viktoria's continued thread of performing rightly. How strong were Viktoria's needs, Claire questioned? Once the deed had been achieved and the rampant passion spent, Claire and Juria had survived without any blood being shed.

Claire trusted that Viktoria, with great effort indeed, did have the ability to staunch her grisly, demanding lust for another's vital body fluids. Claire trusted Viktoria to treat her and Juria with a bit of dignity.

Claire presumed that Viktoria would relent and a ménage would not occur again. She had no guarantees of this but even so, felt it to be so. Once communicated to Viktoria, the same would be communicated to Juria; no more erotic encounters between the three of them.

Her faith sank deep where Juria was concerned. She recognized that he would comply with her wishes; he loved her so. If not, well, that would be dealt with as it occurred.

So, as Juria found several damp leaves a distance away to clean himself with, Claire spoke with Viktoria. They both panted slightly from their exertions and Viktoria had her eyes closed, gorgeous breasts rising and falling with her every inhalation and exhalation, nipple tips remaining dark, rigid and long from the cold as much as the prior ecstasy.

"Viktoria, I need you to hear me and let my words resound into that soft spot that I know exists in you for me, Juria and the children.

I loved what just transpired between the three of us. It meant so much to me that you would engage so deeply with us and, at the same time, bring no harm to us. Many, many thanks sweet Viktoria for that.

But I must preserve my marriage. I love Juria without reserve and he me.

I am certain of that, even as he still feels the pain of his first wife's demise and their shared memories prior to that horrific event. I would die if I lost Juria's present desire for me. Please then, gracious vampire, allow our marriage to remain forever.

I request that we have no more encounters of this kind.

I say this as one decent being to another. Find your means to live as you need but please, for God's sake, and I know that you knew Him once, maybe even a bit now, spare Juria, me and the children the heartache and destruction that your intimate intrusions would most assuredly bring about.

For that alone, I will forever cherish and love you."

Her eyelids languorously opened and Viktoria smiled broadly into Claire's radiant face. Claire understood that Viktoria observed Claire's radiance even in the extreme black of early morn.

"I have struggled in manners harsh and unknown to others. To be undead, not at one's own choosing, is beyond others ability to even remotely comprehend. I have rebelled at its laws and generally have had to give in to those frighteningly fierce urges. Even now the hunger licks at my innards and bites at the base of my brain.

Viktoria went on. "Yet you are correct lovely Claire in that with an omnipotent effort, I can manage to skirt my surging appetite and do what is sensitive and, for the entire world, hugely estimable. And what that is, is to care about beings beyond an exclusive consideration of myself. I grow in joy each time that I experience empathy and overcome my baser needs; like now, in the dark forest with you and Juria.

More. "Ordinarily, I am so eager to slash throats upon my and their immanent climax that I collapse into a fury of violent acts. It is not thought, it just is. And I am always so relieved when I have briefly banished my outsize, always lurking, appetite because I know that I am more me then and less the craving detestable one. I feel not only a bond with you and Juria but I also will prove to myself that I am still part human and not entirely monster by assisting you in Hansel and Gretel's search.

More still. "And so, yes, I spared your lives. I do not always want to be alone, dominant and feared. For that, I will honor your request and will never pursue you or Juria as intimate partners again. Your marriage is safe with me."

Claire clasped Viktoria's hand then and gently pulled her off the flattened grass where they had all lain.

Juria had returned and Claire was desperate for him to understand her viewpoint.

She released Viktoria's hand as Viktoria stood upright and gripped Juria's upper arm so that she could lead him away and speak together out of Viktoria's earshot.

"Juria, I love you passionately and with all of my heart. This incident went beyond me as I discern that it went beyond you in addition. Come hold me while I whisper in your ear the remainder."

Juria came and held her wondrous nudity.

"I could not endure another such episode. I need you too much to take that risk ever again. And Viktoria promised me that she would cease any and all efforts to ever again begin a sexual joining of the three of us. She desires, for her own reasons, the preservation of our marriage. As do I!"

"As do I!" Juria exclaimed.

They all redressed then in what they still had and went forth.

Chapter 26

In Retrospect

He wiped the mixed juices off his flaccid penis. The moist leaves served their purpose fairly well and his genitals were mostly cleaned.

He was ready to redress and restart their pursuit of Hansel and Gretel's kidnapper. He did not want to sort out what had just transpired unless it could be done quickly and effectively. His marriage to Claire was paramount! All else paled totally in comparison.

He had an all-consuming notion, even certainty that Claire believed identically. In retrospect, the just concluded coupling was a delightful luxury that could only be afforded the one time. Once might have been too much. More than once and the luxury would definitely turn to devastation.

Juria returned to a hushed conversation between Claire and Viktoria.

As he approached them and their shining beauty in this midnight hour, he marveled at their contrasts. The dark and light shades and its juxtaposition side by side made their lush forms even more so than they were individually. Simply viewing these two beings unclothed was a heady experience. His cock firmed some as he neared.

Nonetheless, if Claire would have him and his need for her singly, he would swoon and praise God evermore.

He then tucked Viktoria's amazingly shapely form into deep mental recesses where he would not venture henceforth. He looked askance at Viktoria's now standing form one final time.

Suddenly, Claire was at his elbow, throwing words of love and monogamy forever his way. Once led to a distance away, Claire aggressively leaned in to him, kissed his ear and then tickled it with continued words of passion and bonding. Even if he had not already decided, he would have dissolved into her bosom then and given her anything.

He held her, had to have her close; experienced her naked breasts and long nipples as they seared his skin. Out loud, he affirmed his eternal wish to be hers and hers alone.

Viktoria poured herself back into her feathery light and nearly see through raiment.

Juria worked viciously in this moment to suppress her appeal to him. Her jutting breasts hardly hidden by her bodice and her too tiny ass made it nearly impossible for him to focus. Yet he had the perfect solution in his darling Claire.

She too had replaced her attire; what remained of it at least. The tattered cloth intended to cover the full rise of her breasts did not hide anything of her torso from his wanton and widening eyes. Actually, Claire's bounty and forthright beauty eased Juria from his dilemma. When thoughts of sex came to him, he had no difficulty fixating on Claire, not Viktoria.

And, supremely, love towered above form at all times. This sentiment firmly centered itself in him now.

Juria reclaimed his position trailing Viktoria and Claire did the same trailing Juria. They resumed their hectic pace through the thick brush as time vanished in the pause had to somehow be recaptured. Juria's ever active mind spiked visions of Hansel and Gretel's torture extended for the reason that they had all indulged their passions and had delayed the quest thereby.

Juria castigated himself that the time elapsed dedicated to their play might also become the very cause that the children would experience harm. He was shaken strongly and was not able to dispel a vision of imminent doom speeding toward his son and daughter. If that interlude became crucial to their wellbeing, he would roast hotly in the extremes of guilt and sorrow.

Viktoria seemed to have inexhaustible reserves of core energy as she rarely ceased. But of course, she was the undead; supernaturally capable they were.

Exhaustion's shadow already drifted over Claire. She placed a goodly portion of her weight upon Juria as the wending continued. That she leaned her bulk against him reinforced his urgency in locating and rescuing the children.

How had they not found them yet?

For hours, there had been an absolute dearth of signs of their whereabouts. He called for Viktoria to halt.

"What powers do you have that are beyond my feeble capabilities to unearth their location? You have an array of those powers that would shorten this journey of ours and bring them back to Claire and me. Use them now, whatever they might be and whatever cost they may have to us all. That sounds shrill and arrogant, I know. Hansel and Gretel are not yours. But you recognize how precious they are!

Claire will not manage much longer without true rest, any food and enfolding warmth. You can withstand the cold perpetually, she cannot. Please, I implore you. We need you immediately."

His plea brought this response from Viktoria: "My ability to project into the future regarding your offspring has been blocked, thwarted almost completely. I get a tick or two that breaks through the barrier on occasion. Those flash visions are gone within the instant and they leave me, at the most, with the dimmest of possibilities. There is no genuine clarity with them. And I cannot remember them for long. I can neither place any location nor any being or creature that might have them at their mercy. I have flown over the entire woods, penetrated its canopy and spied nothing; not a clue, not a hint of them seems to exist. I do not smell their blood either. They have frustrated me absolutely.

So what, my tender Juria, would you have me do that I have not done already?"

"Fly once again. Reconnoiter the area once more. They cannot have gone beyond the confines of the forest, could they?"

He rested his head upon Claire's shoulder as they all stood in place. "Claire, what do you say? Say anything. We might find knowledge in the most creative of suppositions! It is not real that they have disappeared as if swallowed."

Viktoria took flight into the fading night.

They walked, but not far as Claire slumped to the ground. "I cannot go further!"

Juria sat next to her, supporting her in any manner that he could.

Then the feeblest of sounds came upon them.

Chapter 27

Out of the Shadows

The Guardian had been riveted to the impromptu sexual antics that leaped out at him. He groaned as if a rounded bullet had rent his hide and pierced his gut, leaving it butchered and oozing bloody bits of himself.

He was terrified that in their tumult, he would miss a nuance and fail to preserve Claire's life. Viktoria was incredibly swift and extremely potent once moved to kill.

He tensed on all fours; a routine posture but for the unaccustomed tightness throughout his body. His muscles were at the hair trigger ready, pouncing upon Viktoria before she could do injury to Claire. His acuity was compromised also by his eager animal excitement to join in the passion tussle with them.

His lupine cock had involuntarily unsheathed itself and was long and taut against his belly. It was so heavy though that he strained to tighten his muscles there in order to fix it in position and not let it hang lower and slow his possible attack. He did not know how long he could hold it parallel to his underside. The cock attached to his beastly self was too large when it was fullest. It was almost fullest now.

The insistent throb there, the further elongation as he continued to observe, the pleasurable pain as it stretched and grew swollen, the intermittent and uncontrollable jerking contractions as the tableau of Viktoria, Claire and Juria blended seemed to have cooked his brain and sapped his coiled strength.

The contradictory pulls on him, the requirement of objective vigilance versus consuming lust, racked his hirsute body with shivers beyond his control. As wolf or man, this was too much to ask of any creature.

And the crossover time was approaching quickly. Soon his hide would become skin, his bones would rework themselves, the convolutions of his mind would adjust to human form, his cock would distract less and he would be nude again.

The Guardian was well aware that Viktoria must make haste away from the grasp of the new morning sun's rays also.

He forced himself to hold just barely longer. The moment of climax was upon them and him. His stressed muscles shook and trembled, his cock dropped a bit as he yielded to its burden, and then he heard Viktoria and Juria as they cried out simultaneously. His cock was so red and stretched.

They were releasing. Viktoria's lips gripped Juria's manhood; her throat swallowed over and over, hard, liquid still oozed from her mouth corners.

He viewed Viktoria's legs as they clamped around Claire's ears. He heard Claire panting as Viktoria bucked into Claire's nearly engulfed face.

The Guardian was poised to discharge his own. He contained himself with great effort. He had to know that Claire was safe before he was swept away. It was only after Juria had been pinioned by Claire's ferocious want to give way to her own intense pleasure that the Guardian spurted thick white ropes into the brush.

Time was of the absolute essence for Viktoria as he realized the dawn became imminent. The Guardian sensed the almost palpable tension of his incipient change and realized Viktoria felt more. The lethal nature of burning dawn heat upon Viktoria would turn her into blown, charred flesh; so terminal was this that the undead life transformed instantly into a blink that was scattered far and wide.

So he saw Viktoria and Claire intensively speak a moment. He observed Juria and Claire do likewise, hugging one another in such love that pleased him ever so. She had to transform now and depart or it would be too late! And that was exactly what she did.

Viktoria donned her bats wings, bat face and extended claws and catapulted into the still dark heavens.

Now it was his turn.

His body converted into a sack of grinding and shattering bone, hanks of fallen animal hair, a telescoping and vanishing tail, a shrinking human sized cock and a mind that commanded him to rise upright and balance himself immediately. His nudity required him to race to his nearest appropriate cache of items.

His second priority was to find something for Claire, Juria too, to eat and drink. Their hunger and thirst had to be slaked and satisfied.

Food was not difficult to fetch; water was only fractionally more complex. He planned on retrieving his empty leather pouch from the cache in addition to his clothes and strips of salted, dry venison for the two. The pouch would be filled from the small stream near this particular hiding place of his.

He did all of this within an hour; the hour each day when Claire was most vulnerable without his vigilance. This could not be helped though.

He was clothed, had his water-filled pouch slung over his shoulder and venison wrapped in brilliantly colored green leaves.

Upon his return to the pair's trysting spot, he followed their clear path of broken and repositioned low lying branches. He found them close at hand; Claire in obvious dissolve as Juria cradled her head in the crook of his arm and kissed her gently on her face, touching tears away as they spilled onto her cheeks. Her eyes were occasionally closed.

The Guardian was very satisfied to be on the verge of rescuing them.

"Ma'am, sir, what is the distress here?" the Guardian asked as he kneeled down to their level.

"Can I be of help?" he further probed.

The Guardian took no offense as Juria glimpsed into his eyes. The Guardian hoped that Juria understood the kindness. Juria shuddered in what the Guardian took to be tired relief.

Juria plead this, "Please good sir, my wife is, without doubt, completely done in. We have had little to drink and virtually nothing to eat for several days. My head is swirling so that I cannot even remember how many it has been. We are beyond exhaustion. Do you have anything at all to spare us?"

"My small load should be enough to see you both back on your feet. Here is water."

"Thank you for your generosity. It can do nothing but bring us back to our senses . . . hope restored." With that, Juria took the leather container from the Guardian's outstretched hand and let Claire sip first. Claire was wise enough to simply wet her tongue and lips to begin. Then she swished it inside her mouth. She drew it down her throat after. And she beamed.

"That small amount was delicious; so cold and refreshing. Truly, it is our delight at meeting you."

The Guardian held out the leaf wrapped meat as Juria swigged his portion of the water. Claire took the package and questioned, "For us?" with a quizzical expression.

"Have as much as you need of it. Obviously, your health is at stake. And I partook very recently."

The Guardian ceased to kneel and placed his rear on a bald and dusty patch of ground. The warmth sank into his buttocks. He relished Claire and Juria's silent consumption of his proffering's.

It was premature for him to reveal himself to them. That would occur later.

Chapter 28

Stalked the Wood

From night's womb to casket's tomb, Viktoria made the transition, one place to the other, without distress.

She had pressed herself into a potentially disastrous situation by hesitating even when nocturnal vestiges faded. She lingered in her dalliance at length; that delirious passion bound state whose tentacles could have snuffed her out.

She discerned how treacherous and beguiling sexual transgressions with certain beings were. And it was not the acts of desire so much as it was the relinquishing of control to the all-consuming emotional enmeshment that gave up sight of time and reason.

But was it truly a transgression for Viktoria to have completely quenched her thirst from pleasure's vessel? Yes, for certain, it had been a mistake as she had nearly annihilated herself in having become slave to the heaving, yet caressing and beautiful sensations of bodily interweaving's with the so sexy Claire and Juria. Having yielded to that rampant desire once, Viktoria had learned a magnificently sad lesson that vulnerability was a deceitful charmer with an often lethal bite.

So, as agreed with Claire, their ménage was not to transpire again, ever! Viktoria had determined this before Claire had spoken while she had lingered on the warm, crushed grass beneath her gently prickling, highly receptive skin. Her legs had still been spread in the afterglow of the exchange of the three of them.

But she had roused herself finally, realized her danger and had flown without heed back to home and casket where she drifted into unconsciousness; these last reflections coming and then going swiftly.

Over and over, as waking functions ceased, vague and nebulous images careened inside the curved walls of her skull.

The image was persistent, though, and would distill itself vividly out of all the floating carnival. A faint blue tint revolved roundly upward at a pace frustrating in its sluggish speed and sharp suspense. The blue was so vivid and startling in its immediacy for her. Gradually, the blue hue divided into two halves, one half, the lower half, was mottled with fingers of white while the other half, the upper half, deepened into a raw and cold impression, and remained completely blue.

The white mottling shifted, faded, and coalesced then into misty skyward reaching tendrils. It was very early morning and gently dispersing fog was hanging onto a lake's utterly still surface.

Viktoria sensed the gathering morning heat in spite of the mild chill breeze which disturbed the landscape. The vapor was lifting, melting and her inner vision further observed the entire panorama of purest low lying mountain fed vast pool of water gleaming in crystalline sapphire shades. The knowledge of it being mountain fed came by the fact that she saw the silhouette of snow encrusted peaks looming behind. The sun's orb was yet locked behind those rocky crags.

Out from the wilderness birds arose. The scene then zoomed in upon the aloft creatures. How many were there? The image blurred and angled away rapidly. Focus, go back, view them, what are they really? Rumbling inside that pulsing head of hers, she knew that identifying the birds was the key; yet her mind's perversity blurred more, only to envision wings in flight, nothing beyond that. At least, would she, could she hold onto that thread?

The casket vibrated softly as Viktoria's comatose body intensively trembled while she sought the solution to her recurrent dream.

The energy drained when she was supposedly lying passively and that depletion of energy was enough to insure that her appetite would be monumental upon awakening. Her arteries automatically expanded into pipes that would insist upon being satisfied as soon as she lifted her tomb's cover. This primal craving was further heightened by that familiar surge of wantonness expressed by aching nipples, a hard pulsing clitoral knot and a juiced cleft. And this was in spite of the oh so recent tryst with Claire and Juria.

For one who worshipped at the shrine of control and domination, paradoxically, Viktoria was absolutely captive to so many of her own vampire cravings.

The orb dropped and Viktoria arose.

She set her daytime mental meanderings aside in order to drench her organs in blood. Her arms converted into webbed wings and her body slid into her ugly, aerodynamic desmodic shape. The air served her needs quite well as she scanned territory and situations as proficiently as if she shuffled a deck of cards once and in that amount of time knew each individual card's location within the deck. She was amazingly nimble and deadly accurate as bat.

And, in all of this, she had not forgotten to survey for Hansel and Gretel in all that she soared over.

Rich blood was not necessary this meal. She just required plentiful amounts of the ruby cast fluid. Animal then was as viable a source as human. She was in a hurry and was in no mood to be particular. A bulky, slow and plodding four legged victim to exsanguinate was the ideal here.

Below her was a loosely tethered horse, calmly nibbling on whatever clumps of grass that it could find with head bent sharply down. No rider or equipage at all sat upon its broad back. She guessed that it was of the breed Holsteiner and principally bore the heavy agricultural labor outside of the forests.

So why was the horse here in the forest then? And where was its human companion? A hasty perusal of the larger confines revealed no person nearby. It was almost as if someone had been kind enough to charitably donate one of its livestock to her; the better for her to be promptly on her way. She inwardly chuckled at this notion. She really had no concern whatsoever except to assuage her thirst.

She swooped down to the equine neck, lanced the thick skin with her fanged teeth and drew in sustenance. The animal was struck dumb, senseless and dead in an instant. It fell to its forward shanks and then rolled to its side in eternal submission. Viktoria flapped her wings as she fed, fused to the red rush that not only reduced her hunger but eased the sexual urge as well.

Finished, the animal corpse without a remaining drop, Viktoria stealthily launched herself away from the carnage she had created.

She pictured the rider as he came upon his gored mount; he would be on foot from here on out. She was pleased with what seemed to her a wry sense of humor.

As she rode the updraft, parallel motion far away caught at her peripheral vision.

She paid scant attention to it initially but then her dream sprang upon her. And because of that, she focused intently on the disappearing object. Her swiftness had most certainly surprised the other. But that was it! The dream was solved. Birds they were not. She had just now seen what it was.

It was the mirror image of her. The dream had shown her two bats, herself and one other. The dream had nudged her perfectly toward an awareness she otherwise would have missed. Now she knew realities truth and that truth was going to be very challenging.

There was another vampire bat who claimed the sky along with Viktoria. And that further meant another of the undead stalked the wood.

Chapter 29

Thresholds Tossed Aside

She calmly observed Henry's confusion as she spoke those two words to him. He had never met her, yet she guessed that at some stage in Juria and Claire's intimacy, Henry and Adelaide had been shown the calotype prints of her. Juria had insisted that she be photographed. It was a new, cumbersome and expensive process; he had been so proud of those copies of her though. They must be yellowing, moldering by now.

The light of recognition came into his eyes.

She smiled sweetly as she explained her miraculous presence. "Hansel and Gretel have been at my side for several days now. And yes, one of their parents is right here."

Adelaide gasped as she simultaneously raised her head from the children's embrace. "Oh my God, dear, you are not dead!"

"Not to frighten you or Henry upon our first meeting but, to be specific, I am undead."

Hansel and Gretel pulled on Henry's sleeve and then Hansel blurted out, "Don't be so frightened of Mama! Please don't be scared of her Grandpapa, Grandmama! Isn't she beautiful?"

It was obvious to Danika that Adelaide and Henry were softened on the spot as Hansel used those endearments regarding them. Danika was cognizant of the fact that Gretel cared about the older pair equal to

Hansel; there was an ecstatic flush on both children's cheeks that was impossible to miss. And they had talked incessantly of their Grandpapa and Grandmama over their last several days' adventure.

Danika did not mind this whatsoever.

She sensed the quality of the couple in the warmth and joy in their enfolding hugs of her son and daughter.

They were not blood to Hansel and Gretel but that was ignored by the children. She would ignore that too. Her mother's heart beat with pleasure that was so big that it momentarily eclipsed her vampire's heart and pushed it into a timid shadow.

Just prior to arriving here, Danika had scouted the area to assure herself that their path to the estate was clear and unencumbered.

Disaster had nearly struck in a second of sudden and profound astonishment.

She had been airborne, with the children patiently awaiting her return in their den, when alarm had enveloped her completely. She had almost ceased breathing and beating her wings altogether. She had even commenced a plunge right out of the sky before correcting herself and swooping away from the other bat with maximum quickness.

She should have been prepared for all possibilities but her confidence in not having been discovered for days put her at an unwarranted ease. And the carelessness of having not anticipated Viktoria's presence, her greatest threat to success, was unforgiveable. But there Viktoria had been; outlined in the sky's distance. Danika prayed to the gods of the undead that she had gone unnoticed.

She, Hansel and Gretel were soon to be sheltered at the estate with Adelaide and Henry. Her inexplicable gaffe had not been beyond repair it seemed. She was, though, still furious at herself for the happening.

But she needed to focus. Her next order of business was to quell Adelaide and Henry's fears about her rebirth as a vampire. That was diplomacy and grace that she was very capable of; even if not all of these sweetened words were entirely true.

"I can only imagine your consternation and disbelief here. Juria considered me very, very dead. And I am very apologetic to you, your daughter, and your son-in-law that I performed this deception.

Abandoning Hansel and Gretel temporarily was the most trying and troubling aspect of all.

Juria and I had excitedly discussed the life of the undead many a time in our marriage. It was a bit of fascination for both of us; much more so me than Juria as it turned out. My curiosity and obsession built. At a point in our discussion, Juria indicated his ultimate discomfort in continued exploration of the subject. His fright and concern for the children left him unwilling. And then he blocked it completely from his mind.

I never said more to him from then on but it was a rift as I fantasized the riches of eternal existence more and more. As you can probably surmise, it gripped me and I pursued it.

As Juria would sleep, I would sneak out into the cradle of the night. The night seemed boon to me and it proffered itself to my wishes one late wandering eve. My neck was slashed and rent with two gore holes affixed.

This I am sure that you were told at some point. That is how the search party came across me; apparently lifeless and beyond help.

Juria grieved tremendously. I was well aware of that but was now a pawn in my own web of desires. Eternal life beckoned for me then. I thought of nothing else and quivered with an unholy anticipation of that eternal life.

Juria had my corpse laid on a slab at our cottage in the wood with a velvet burial cloth draped over me. My wounds were only at my neck; all else remained physically the same. Juria was so dumbstruck in his torment that he failed to see that I was glowing preternaturally and was not decomposing one iota.

As he dug my grave outside, I fled, fled into the wonder of a new and enchanted life. I remain fully enamored of this life to this day.

He collapsed for many a day once my body mysteriously vanished. I realize this because I have returned often to my family. I always came and went unrevealed. I just wanted to assure myself of their health and safety. I was assuaging a deep river of guilt also.

Several days ago, the children wandered in the forest. In my rescue of them, I have decided to make my return permanent."

Everyone remained rapt as Danika spun out her words. An incredulous silence hung over Adelaide and Henry and they stared at the gorgeous being before them blankly.

Adelaide finally found her voice. "Please, won't you all step inside and partake of our hearth and home."

Henry nodded his assent.

Danika gracefully swept past the older couple into the manors interior.

The children did no such thing. They burbled to Henry and Adelaide as they noisily frolicked through the entryway and into the plush comfort of their Grandparent's home.

Adelaide and Henry loved the fact that the children were now underfoot. Their presence gave off such a vibrant energy that the couple's abode felt intensively lived in at this moment.

Chapter 30

Last Ditch Effort

The water was revitalizing to Claire and the dried strips of meat lifted her supremely weary spirits to the point that she even supposed that she could carry on shortly.

Before the stranger appeared, she had been concerned that she might give way and perish in her own wooded neighborhood with her thoroughly exhausted husband at her side.

The irony of being so near to home and yet a victim without recourse had lashed at her. The greater insult was that she would have expired without any reassurance either of Hansel and Gretel's status or of having a last opportunity to tell them of her love and concern for them.

Her entire being pulsed gratitude toward the man who assisted them in their travail.

"You are a godsend that we deserved but absolutely did not expect," Claire choked out as she and Juria chewed hard and swallowed often.

He beamed her direction especially as she and Juria's revival progressed.

She, of a sudden, averted her eyes from his, tucked chin to chest, rounded her shoulders and thereby attempted to shield herself from him as she grasped at her hopeless bodice. There was virtually no material left there and she recognized that her efforts to cover herself were in vain.

She proceeded to fiddle with the remnants nonetheless.

She did not care to incite lasciviousness on his part. Juria performed his part for her fully. Of that, she was happy.

He slid over to her, draped a large arm over her hunched back and interrupted the stranger's gaze with a sharp look of his own. She no longer felt as exposed or vulnerable as she had just moments before.

"We thank you profusely. How did you come upon us? And do we owe you anything in return?" Claire asked with extended thrust of head from her shielded and curled form.

Juria glared at length at this interloper in spite of being rescued by him. Juria would protect his woman at all costs, Claire knew.

The stranger introduced himself. "It was an innocent encounter, I assure you. And neither of you owe me anything. You were in dire straits and I was able to accommodate you. You would have done the same had roles been reversed, I am sure.

I have traveled through this wood often. I farm to the east and trade to the west with this wood in between. How do the two of you find yourself here, and in this obvious predicament? Can I possibly be of further help?"

Claire had not the first inkling that the Guardian told these lies, and told them in well prepared smoothness, because he wanted to develop a fragment of trust between them prior to unwinding the truth of his position and presence here.

Claire turned to face Juria; his face giving back a mien of slight acquiescence to the stranger's offer of aid.

"Do you happen to have any large cloth that I could wrap around myself? My dirndl, as you certainly can witness, was not meant to be worn at length in a grueling forested search for my Stepchildren, his children."

"Absolutely!

It is my stupidity in not offering you something of this kind immediately. I can do much better than you request. I have several wool sweaters in my pack with which you can wear to defend yourself against exposure to the chill, scratches and tears from the larger brush and from examinations undesired.

I am stunned, from the sounds of what you have briefly said, that you were not in breakdown much earlier. You both must be very capable and durable individuals."

Claire was pleased by the gift of the heavy sweater. She placed it over her head and chest. The fit was tight where her bulging breasts protruded but was slack and loose at her wasp waist.

Claire was not a fashion maven here and now and simply valued the comfort afforded by the garment.

Her modesty was appeased in addition. Leering glances at what she realized were her extremes of feminine proportions bothered her immensely.

To be a woman in a man's world, a woman of substance, high ability and intelligence with a perfect shape, well that perfect shape was a burden, a hindrance and an aspect that angered her. That shape was certain to get her better qualities dismissed and her body hungrily chased. Achieving a delicate balance, so as to not offend sensibilities in that regard, required modesty in vast doses.

This modesty she mustered but her anger flared at the grotesque unfairness of the oppressive behaviors she experienced constantly.

That she even harbored such radical opinions as this would put her in abruptly grave societal danger if she were to ever express them aloud.

She cherished Juria much, as his was a very open and facilitating outlook toward her; she wore and bore no chains due to Juria.

Inexplicably, Claire was struck with an idea; an idea so obvious that its presence had escaped everyone. If Hansel and Gretel could not find their way back to the small homestead of theirs, possibly they could find their way to her parent's estate. Henry and Adelaide would shelter the children without a doubt!

And then send a messenger to their cottage . . . where Juria and Claire were not.

Claire wrenched Juria upward and yelled out "Let's go!"

Claire thought to herself, what better last ditch effort than pouncing upon her beloved father and mother.

Beyond that, if the children were there, Claire and Juria would relieve them of anxiety about their separation from the children.

The stranger lunged forward with them as if to follow. And then he vanished.

Precisely then, circle of sun having tracked below the horizon, Viktoria swung in front of their striding party and instantaneously transposed to woman.

Chapter 31

Focused Trek

As Viktoria turned from creature to luscious woman, the stranger, who had but a moment ago stepped along with them, veered off into the brushy thickets and went thoroughly missing.

Day's luminosity was fully spent.

Juria was not able to tell in movement, expression or word if Viktoria had detected the departing individual. No matter as there was much to impart to Viktoria as fast and furiously as possible.

As it was Claire's idea, Juria resisted his urge to speak. Claire explained to Viktoria thus, "Come Viktoria, come and we will all find our way to my parent's estate. It is there that Juria and I believe that we will locate Hansel and Gretel. It is shelter for them.

And, according to Juria, Hansel has a vague knowledge of the direction there through this timberland; presuming that he is not disoriented by now."

Viktoria blocked the two of them from hastening past her. "Hold! What of the kidnapper? That villain might have their own notions of where to haul, and then hide, them. What is your rational regarding that?

What if he cared not a bit for the suggestion of the estate?"

Juria seized this pause to leap into the space between words.

He responded for Claire. "The rhyme and the reason for focusing our trek upon arriving at the estate are nothing more than a logical hunch and, in addition, that all of our other options have proved fruitless. We have floundered detecting them in spite of your powers, your airborne surveillance, my woodsman's expertise, Claire and my dogged and sustained efforts to the point of her collapse earlier; none of that has given us more than several sparse and hazy clues.

A kidnapper would easily comprehend the advantage of civilized shelter, available food, warmth and the peace to plan further. It is the best we have.

Our hope is that you join us further for we value your desire to aid us. We go, though, to the estate regardless. So, please, yield immediately and let us pass!"

She did just that. She let Claire and he pass. Then she fell in behind.

A sliver of puzzlement lanced at Juria's brain as he, Claire and Viktoria proceeded forward.

As he furrowed his brows, he had inadvertently clomped ahead of Claire but now let her stride past him as she excitedly anticipated the passage to the estate.

Juria also felt the heat and intensity of Viktoria trailing him. He definitely enjoyed being squeezed between the two lovely women. He was mindful of Viktoria's intermittent gaze upon his ass and that intuitive certainty sent tender, flashing shivers through his body.

He loved the titillation that his fantasies of Viktoria and Claire's voluptuous mounding breasts especially brought to his now quivering and slightly stiffening manhood. He imagined that the women, his wife one and the darkly lustrous other, would be capable of rousing a dead man into deeds of energy and excess. He wondered if possibly

Viktoria's powers had already granted her this experience. He smiled wryly at this picture.

But his original perplexity returned.

Why had he, Juria, not undergone pangs of jealousy as their threesome had joyfully progressed into its blissful conclusion while the slightest overture of the stranger on the path toward Claire had whipped up immediate and intense animosity? Should not Claire entwined with Viktoria have incited his wrath and have provoked him into sudden exclamations for all three to cease? Should not the stranger's generosity and lifesaving acts toward both of them have inspired a grateful response on his part?

And what of the stranger's possibly desirous glances at what was a lushly inviting and bounteous tableau of prominent, pendulously hung, and perfectly formed breasts, shifting in nipple display as threadbare bodice material shredded more and more? Juria had lusted to finger and play with those tender, sensitive, long nipples of Claire's while they had been visible. The stranger's reaction had been absolutely reasonable.

Juria's relief at the stranger's vanishing though was equally as reasonable. Juria did not want to share Claire with another man! That notion was intolerable to him. He loved Claire ceaselessly and infinitely. To share his wife with a man, never!

He had just done the same with a woman though. Well, he presumed, and he was attempting to be totally honest with himself, he could not conceive of Claire abandoning him for a woman. Oh how he underestimated the force of women. He suffered shame at his occasional unfair and skewed opinions.

What a bastard! It was the very strength of his shame that pressed him past giving deeper analysis to the seemingly immoveable belief. What he was willing to continue to ponder was that he was captivated and charged beyond his control when they all coupled.

What a selfish being he was! He had allowed Viktoria's allure to sway him beyond reason. He and Claire agreed that it would never happen again. Viktoria, bless her dark vampire heart, concurred fully with him and Claire in this regard.

But, and Juria grinned widely at this, nothing would ever keep him from replaying their threesome repeatedly in the safe confines of his head.

The three of them had consumed much distance all the while that he had pondered his gross flaws and gravely inconsistent views of sex and marriage.

Juria was content though to permit his imperfections to settle beneath the focus of arriving at the estate and checking in with Claire's parents; that, Juria inwardly cringed, was not going to proceed easily. Henry and Adelaide had not managed to disguise their dislike and disappointment towards him from the onset of his and Claire's connection.

They had tried since to reverse their estimation of him he knew but they had failed miserably; Henry so much more so than Adelaide as Henry's impatience with and dismissal of all that Juria did vibrated constantly on Henry's surface.

Adelaide sided with Henry even when she had misgivings and disagreements with him. She was a good and dutiful wife as Claire had informed Juria to the point of his exhaustion.

Juria had done all that he could to bring a positive bloom to his relationship with the older pair. He had ripped himself apart internally to submit to their requirements and he would do it no further. Juria intended to maintain his pride this time around.

Heeding surroundings now, Juria judged that they were closing in upon their destination.

Dawn was near to shearing the midnight curtain into a pile of haphazard folds at their feet. Incipient light was readying its assault upon them.

Viktoria altered herself and swept back to her lair where her coffin lay. The fever of day was upon them. Quiet and calm was about to depart.

Chapter 32

Ambivalence Set Aside

She and Henry were almost as proud of their estate as they were their child and step grandchildren. She periodically amused herself with whimsical reflections as she valued no item remotely with her beloved Hansel and Gretel.

Adelaide and he had resided on these grounds their entire marriage. The estate was his from inheritance. He had supported their lifestyle with the same vigor as his father had for his wife. And they relied on no one.

How would she describe the place? It was a lordly place whose details were thoroughly etched in fond and lengthy memory.

The manor house itself, of course, was her most cherished of the multiple structures comprising their full abode. The house was crafted in a spacious baroque style that was ornate but hardly elaborate. Adelaide was a modest woman. The effect of chiaroscuro predominated and she was often held spellbound as the shadow competed with its contrast of vivid light and radiant color.

The floors were created exclusively in a marble that gave Adelaide a sense of solidity that was profound and gratifying. The oak windows were surrounded by marble sills supported by the sturdiest of thick wood walls. The terrace, situated with a warm southern exposure, allowed a valley view that was comprehensive and magnificent in its panorama of verdant green pine and the occasional sparkle of sun dappled river water.

She treasured the fact that the house contained both an upper and lower floor.

The main entrance, where all stood momentarily, held a pantry. The vast kitchen with its complete array of the oft used cooking, serving and eating utensils, even included a smaller breakfast room with its own entrance permitting private access to the second floor.

Breaking the uniformity of marble and rich wood loomed the massive brass banisters.

The bedrooms, guestrooms, balconies and a gallery flooded the second floor.

How could she, Henry also, not be more than delighted with their dwelling?

The manor house was simply the largest of the constructions organized around a central courtyard and lush garden. Peppered in a circle, there stood this, the most northerly structure, then a small and tidy church with cemetery directly west, next an even tinier distillery directly east and also the stables on a rigid line south. Filling the gaps in the ring were a private guesthouse, housekeeper and cook's quarters, a wonderfully producing vineyard and a riding arena that butted up against the stables.

She was loath to bring anyone into this sacred circumference unless she was assured of their positive intent and rational character. She and Henry had discussed this issue multiply. Neither desired risking their sanctuary in the interest of welcoming unknown, untested individuals.

Hansel and Gretel were adored and esteemed. What of Danika though? Yet Henry stepped aside for all three. Adelaide did also, reluctantly. All indicators were flashing caution signals Adelaide's way. She, as Henry oft reminded her, had the fatal trait of opened mindedness. So she gazed at Danika with a determined willingness to listen at the least, believe at the most.

They sat themselves in the breakfast room first with the children unable to be still in their glee.

As she sought out morsels for the children to ravenously plunge down their throats, Adelaide prepared to absorb all Danika described.

"I decided to revisit the children several nights ago in my usual invisible fashion. I always require my young brood to be safe, secure, and content. I have done this often after I left Juria. They are my children and I will do everything in my ample power to give them the best of lives.

This last reappearance proved to be supremely eventful. No one was at home upon my arrival. As a vampire, I have psychic abilities that come to me at crucial instants given intent focus on my part. These psychic visuals can be blocked but only when those involved with identical capacities are intentionally blocking the specific other. Both can block one another simultaneously and the proximate visuals and surrounds of each are curbed. It's like fighting with raised and unseen swords. I can cast this at other demons successfully too and have. Ironically, not all undead are apprised of this. One needs to be told or simply be astute to details. Even we are subject to learning. I was told.

So, I brought this force to bear in order to discover Juria, Claire, Hansel and Gretel's location. It was night and they should have been in the cottage. It took just seconds for me to realize that my son and daughter were wayward, and then confined.

They were ignorant of their danger as they slept. I had only seconds to rectify their situation. Their captor was a vampire, who was totally oblivious of me, and so open to my psychic probes of her situation. I realized she arose sluggishly because of brief disorientation from severe dreams.

I braced, rushed into winged shape, smashed through doors and as gently as was possible without losing my grip I grasped Hansel and Gretel with my mouth. They wept but were startled and too fearful to struggle.

I have a virtually bottomless cave that I use when I reappear in this area. That is where I took them. I did not require it as it was night and my time of freedom and locomotion. I coveted an opportunity to tell my tale to my children though and so went to a secure haven with them. I did not desire distraction in this by worry of escaping deadly brightness at first hint of daybreak. I required respite from that concern.

My children were wholly shocked that their Mother lived. They rejoiced even as they became cognizant of my eternal condition."

Danika clasped Hansel and Gretel then. They barely hesitated to kiss and grasp her too. Adelaide could not ignore the seeming joy that they expressed toward each other; yet the pause as well.

Danika continued. "We were not able to comfortably reside in my cave. Obviously, I could, the children could not. It was horribly difficult for them even in the time that we were there. So, we came here and are so glad. Thank you so much."

Out of character, Henry cheerfully clucked at the scene and blushed when Adelaide caught him in the act. "I am so ecstatic that our beloved Hansel and Gretel have survived the span of days and all due to their Mother. It is miraculous.

And that lout Juria! He can't even keep track of his children. He is incompetent! Claire will surely apprehend that after this event!"

Adelaide was not certain of any vampire and that counted Danika. Henry and the children's response to Danika softened Adelaide considerably. As an obedient wife, she should, she would side with Henry.

Adelaide observed as Henry stood up. "You will all stay with us. Danika, you will stay in the guesthouse. It has a basement below it. Make it as you need and require. I have a half dozen pine boxes always prepared for a death on the property. With so many staff, birth and death occur often enough.

You will be able to rely on that to closet yourself away in the day. Hansel and Gretel will enjoy the guestrooms of their usual choosing in the manor house."

The children clapped. Danika sighed appreciatively. Adelaide was still concerned with what could occur were Henry and she ever in disagreement with Danika.

Henry was pleased with himself. Adelaide chose to complement that and set aside her ambivalence toward Danika. It remained lodged but was buried in the fertile soil of her husband's demands.

Chapter 33

His Capitulation As Well

The mixed bag of emotions that Henry experienced as he established the rules of residence for Danika, Hansel and Gretel roiled inside his gut.

Grizzled old bird that he appeared, he was no one's fool! And he had not been taken in by Danika he believed. He was wary of her destructive and violent capabilities when she had donned the cloak of the undead; not only donned it but sought it out avidly and with so much fervor that she had temporarily abandoned her own.

He had to admit that she had circled back and now monitored her children tenaciously.

And, as far as Henry was concerned, Juria needed the oversight much more so than Hansel or Gretel.

He appreciated Danika for her willingness to be truly attentive to the needs of his precious Step grandchildren whom he valued beyond life itself. He was so heartbroken and torn at his own daughter's choice of mate that Danika grew in his estimation astonishingly over Claire. It all became a mash of weltering, warring emotions that inspired no on the spot opinion in him except that Hansel and Gretel were his figurative, sadly not actual, lifeblood and that he respected Danika in a rising tide the longer that he heard her unveiling. He discerned not only her treatment of the children but, he assumed, their profusely loving bond together.

He blushed at the pleasure of it all.

He was no innocent, as Adelaide was, in respect to comprehension of the twilight realm of beasts and monsters. After all, he had set Vincent on the path to protecting his adored yet highly disappointing daughter.

Again, his hatred of Juria bounded and leaped to the forefront for an explosive instant. How could Claire have been so sightless as to have picked Juria for a partner? She was such a gorgeous and well-rounded woman; so many past suitors too. He almost spat as he recollected her choice of the galumphing woodsman.

Henry quickly suppressed this tact as he recognized it would twist him ugly and churlish and, most destructively, out of control. Get a grip old man, he ranted to himself. Back to Vincent then!

Henry had been especially apprised of the hellish ring of damned creatures when Vincent revealed his imprisonment to the ghastly bite of the werewolf. Vincent described minutely the horrors of the changeover and his brute nature as beast.

Immediately, upon Vincent's exposure of himself, Henry put Vincent's fate to use for himself, for his family. For favors given, he had asked Vincent to protect his darling, his deceived and errant Claire, evermore. It was blatantly apparent to all who were not blind that Juria was not fit or able to do this himself for Claire. Bah on that man! So Henry had requested Vincent to keep Claire safe, in perpetuity.

Vincent did not refuse him and had been surreptitiously at Claire's side hence. This relieved Henry no end. It also made him absolutely familiar with the existence of werewolves, vampires, demons and spirits. Henry was frightened of this hell on earth as anyone should and would be. He understood that he would ultimately capitulate to Danika out of the dread of annihilation wrought were he to significantly challenge her at all.

It was then that he made his pronouncement to all gathered in the small breakfast room.

And he spoke so definitely in order to deceive his wife especially. She had to trust him and believe him; continue to believe in him. For doubt to spring into her heart, for her to disagree and defy him in any manner would critically weaken his position with Danika. Danika also must sense only certainty in him as well. Were she to become an adversary, only her perception of his apparent strength would overcome her own strength.

But, ironically, that sense of being charmed by her was gathering momentum such that he was undergoing a friendly attraction to her innate sweetness; blended with that was a potentially catastrophic question burning deep within. What did it feel like to hold the chalice of eternal life close to one's bosom? He wondered awestruck at that.

And he had to stomp it out before it permeated through each and every one of his pores, oozing desire for a grim future. And that was how Danika might win. This possible contagion within him had to be forcibly ripped from his core. Oh God in Heaven help me! He was smothered with this consideration. God only could help him were he to submit to fascination and a craving there.

The project that he had just mentioned was the best salve for his racing mind. "Adelaide, now that Hansel and Gretel are well fed, please put them down for sleep."

"Certainly I will Henry. Hold my hands sweet ones and I will take you to your usual rooms upstairs and tuck you into such warm and cozy beds."

Hansel's eyes glittered. Gretel's grin arched from one tiny ear to the other.

Henry was certain that tiredness would overtake both on the instant that they laid their heads on the well fluffed pillows, had goose down blankets pulled up to their chins and Adelaide had cooed potent lullabies to them.

Danika, applying her level and calm stare at Henry, rose up from her seat. "You will have to excuse me briefly. I am famished and must dine soon. The guesthouse is known to me. I identified it as the three of us attained your doorstep earlier. Kindly leave it unlocked and I will unearth its recesses.

You and Adelaide are truly quite wonderful people. Your sincere and genuine hospitality has eased my heart and soul greatly."

And laughing softly, she continued. "I do have one you know; both actually. Regardless, yours is a loving abode with a welcoming hearth."

"It is our pleasure at having you, to be sure. That you truly are alive and well is incredible. It is one of the chief surprises in all my years. While you are departed, I will see to your living quarters."

They both chuckled at his play on words.

With that, Danika faded from the room, from the entrance and the manor house, from the sky altogether.

Swiftly, Henry paced to the margins of the cemetery where the pine boxes were stored.

He would do this as quietly as he was capable of so that his sleeping staff would not be disturbed. What would they think if they observed him hoisting up a pine box and carrying it over to the private guesthouse? Talk, most certainly, would be plentiful and disruptive.

As he silently performed his task, he did not resist pondering Danika's physical appeal. That she was an auburn beauty with a build that demanded attention created a further concern for Henry. She was tender, sweet, gracious, a superb mother, devastatingly handsome and a vampire. Her package was one that drew even the knowledgeable in. And the final enticement of unlimited longevity was the capper.

He had to resist. The profoundly cruel and primitive aspect there was, truly, more deadly than death. His enthrallment had to be thwarted. He hoped that he was able.

Chapter 34

Goodness Exposed

The Guardian had morphed and dressed already.

Claire's parent's estate was ahead, set atop a plateau that loomed over the wooded vale they presently occupied. That estate simmered against the lit and already overheated sky in regal shape and fluid grandeur.

Soon the three of them, Juria, Claire and he were to begin the ascent onto serpentine road leading to the consolidated community above. Visiting Henry and Adelaide was a favorite pastime of his; or had been before he became shackled to the task of securing all for Claire.

Time was leaning on him though. He had a premonition that his unvarnished, unhidden aid would be required shortly and that they would only enlist his assistance if they were privy to exactly his real identity and genuine function. He was resolute that revelation was an urgent necessity.

They rested and he was in human incarnation; therefore, the perfect instant to step from the overgrowth back onto the trail.

He counted upon their prior meeting to sooth them enough to then be able to convey the truth to them.

His approach was carefully scrutinized. Juria frowned while Claire maintained an open expression; bland but not harsh. He closed the distance in a step that was casual, measured and calm so that he hoped they would feel at greater ease.

"You might be questioning my disappearance and reappearance. That would be very understandable. I apologize for my rapid exit from you both last evening. It was of necessity as is what I am about to divulge to you now."

Juria creased his brow further. Claire elbowed him in the ribs and patted the earth next to her simultaneously. "Relax Juria. I am very curious as to what this mysterious, but generous, stranger may want to say to us."

Juria flinched fleetingly and then clearly unwound. "Sir, sit and reveal to us what you are so evidently aching to spit out."

The Guardian blurted, "I mean the two of you absolutely no harm!"

"Of course not," Juria exclaimed. "Had you meant us injury, you best would have simply let the both of us expire from our exhaustion on the trail a day ago. As you plainly resuscitated us, it would be absurd for us to fear you now. To revive us to then hurt us would be irrational, man. In any case, I am here to defend Claire and myself if you attacked."

"You understand me well but know me not at all, so I shall proceed.

You, Claire, have a guardian, a Guardian that you are not at all cognizant of. You have had this bodyguard for years at your father's bidding.

Does that astonish or puzzle you? It should not in knowing your father. Henry has never been convinced that you were properly defended by Juria.

And Juria, Henry cannot help himself. He knows you not though he still regards you poorly. Therefore, it is not your problem really, rather it is Henry's. He has even let it affect his attitude toward you Claire. He is being unjust to say the least."

"You both glance ironically at me. How do I know all these names, yours included?

I must introduce myself. I am Vincent and a nephew of your father's. You have never met me because your father, as he is with Juria, has always been ashamed of me. I was ashamed of myself at length also.

I owned no land, neither earned nor saved any money, was a no account and a gambler. Beer, whiskey, any alcohol was my beverage of choice. Your father sheltered me when I was at my worst. Blood meant more to Henry than shame, I presume. He permitted me to become sober and healthy.

He taught me the skills of a farmhand and craftsman, then of a manager and then of an owner. He provided me, not as a loan mind you but as a gift, a sum of money from his limitless seeming coffers. He instructed me to buy land and start farming it. I did just that.

He solicited in return only that I someday repay him a favor in his moment of tribulation. Of course, I answered him in the affirmative. He had saved me, remade me and brought a smattering of achievement to my existence. My farm paled next to his estate but that was of minor concern. He was my hero."

The Guardian ceased and wiped his brow, then drew forcefully on his pouch of water and offered it to Claire and Juria as well.

"Tending one of my perimeter fields as dusk rolled into dark, I heard several odd sounds but paid no attention. I had nearly ended my planting of seeds and strained to finish.

Lo, I was being hunted. A wolf, charging in a blur, lunged at one of my stooped shoulders. I curled onto the earth with amazing speed and kicked out at the slavering animal so effectively that I extracted his blood. Unfortunately, he drew mine as well.

He ran as he realized I was no meek meal for him. I was bitten though. And my alteration was swift and without mercy. That very eve, I transformed into a werewolf. Yes, me! It happened as the sun plunged beneath the horizon. My human visage reestablished itself with its rising."

Claire and Juria stood transfixed, rapt as the account unfolded. "But this protector, what became of him?" Claire rasped out.

"I am your Guardian, Claire. I am Vincent and your Guardian.

Previously, you were not ready to witness that in me and still remain collected. That is why I left you on the trail and threw myself out of sight into the brush.

Anyway, onward. When I informed Henry of my sad plight, he was firm. At his demand, I discharged my obligation to him. And that has been to shadow you, Claire, everywhere. It was not what I wished for as I am reasonably certain that the two of you can competently shield one another from damage. Although, the vampire adds a new variable that elevates your peril.

In any event, I disagreed with Henry but was bound to do his bidding."

The Guardian, Vincent, scratched at his chin in a second's repose. "Light is diminishing as I speak. You have borne my saga with patience. I will get you securely to your death Claire, whenever that may transpire. That assumes I survive also. And I will. Almost nothing can cause my demise.

I start to talk in haste as day's end approaches. I have an all-consuming instinct that you will require my presence often, close at your side and with your total cooperation imminently. If I had not exposed my purpose and my goodness to you here and now I would not have received your cooperation and understanding whatsoever. You must also tolerate me in my embodiment as werewolf. So must Viktoria. Since I am only in wolf form at night, and that is when Viktoria ascends to activity, the two of you will have to deliver to her my righteous intent."

Dark was scattering illumination into faint ghosts of its earlier self. Vincent would convert soon.

And Viktoria would turn up presently. It was time for Claire and Juria to bring understanding of his presence to Viktoria.

Chapter 35

Undead Alive

Fraught urges recently quelled, Viktoria drifted nearer to the pair below. With belly stretched and mental energy directed at the elusive other, who was obviously a vampire imposed upon her territory and had laid much ruin to her home and shelter and most likely had the children in thrall too, Viktoria was startled upon alighting to discover three in the party.

That third figure was a behemoth with massive muscled shoulders, sharply pointed snout and ears of the wolf, menacing onyx hued irises, mildly swaying genitals below a huge blunt, hirsute trunk with a whipping, almost frantic tail.

She was not intimidated whatsoever though. She ruled this area and there was no rival who could match her.

Why were Claire and Juria so still and composed in their stance as she strode toward them?

"Do I need to be alarmed at what crouches before me?"

"Absolutely not," Claire proclaimed.

"We have a new companion joining us in our pursuit of Hansel and Gretel. He is an unbelievable ally and as such you should not feel challenged. Threatened you are not as the wolf, Juria and I realize your omnipotence.

Hear me out completely. This narrative will marvel even you. Juria and I were awestruck at the rendition. Now I shall tell you."

From Viktoria, "Do proceed quickly. I comprehend his brute abilities but not the reason for his presence. Enlighten me immediately."

Viktoria listened intently to Claire and Juria's unraveling of all that had befallen the werewolf. It was ironic that she considered him a monstrosity; he was no more that than she. It seemed that there had been a pact between this one and Claire's father. His name was Vincent and his goodwill was vividly conveyed to her.

The werewolf, Guardian, Vincent, what have you, stood immobile during the entire captivating story. He peered into her intently all the while and by his intensity, stirred her undead core. She could now be called the undead alive.

It was these last days that had produced wave upon wave of unanticipated and difficult to channel libidinous sensations. Her vampire's appetite had already been sated. This was raw, sexual energy that spilled from her for no cause greater than the unpretentious fundaments of attraction. It had occurred with Juria and Claire. It was seizing her this instant as she returned Vincent's steady evaluatory look.

Her loins flushed and then gushed. She had to have him somehow and right away. Her web of nipples, clitoris and vaginal opening pulsed shatteringly.

"Enough now, I have heard enough. It is too implausible a tale to be a lie. Who could have, would have, been able to create that whole cloth out of thin air? No, it is the unpredictable workings of real life and its often bizarre machinations."

Viktoria walked toward Vincent with steady and assured pace. She burned in the blazing tinder that crackled between them. The white hot embers shooting skyward flared with each step that brought them closer. Vincent remained seemingly calm but Viktoria recognized this as artifice as he poised statue stiff.

What gave his true reaction away to her, what yielded all that she required was that his growing heavy cock had elongated and crawled from its sheath towards her. She so wanted to pet it. It was such a big organ; a big organ with a glistening sheen forming a clear drop at tips end. She would touch it as nothing else would ever do.

Peripherally, she was certain of Claire and Juria's paralysis. Their wide eyes were fixed on the evolving scene before them.

Looks locked, black on black eyes entranced, frozen in place; Viktoria nearly hissed she was so thrilled. Vincent was poised and quivering fully.

As Viktoria touched his hot and now dripping glans to begin, she was conscious of his quivering changing to a stronger trembling. His cock widened and lengthened, the lengthening impressive as a small telescope into an enormous tube would be. His tube was in her grasp and she clasped his shaft with her encircled hand. Her hand was dwarfed by his cock's girth. Yet her hand did close around this thing when she stretched her palm and fingers with joyous effort.

She heard his breath lightly whistle from between slightly parted wolfish lips. She luxuriated in the incipient avalanche of snapping, tingling, and craving sensation in engorged nipples, dense thudding clit, drowning and alternately sizzling opening.

Finally, as she pumped his column more forcefully, Vincent shuddered and broadened his stance. With one hand, she ripped her bodice in half. Her diaphanous gown fell off of her completely once torn so thoroughly. And her polished, full, dark mounds tumbled down before him.

She pinched one of her wildly itching and thick beckoning nipples. She needed him to growl in his passion. She waited not a whit before she heard that anticipated rich timbered growl. She was afire with lust for him. He pointed the means and the way to fulfillment with his still swelling organ. Even Viktoria was finding that she was mildly timid about fitting that into her. Paradoxically, the thought caused her loins to tremble and her fount to flow copiously more.

She removed her fingers from her hard and jutting nipple. She tentatively dipped her forefinger inside of herself and was shocked at the amount of her sticky sweet juices. She tasted her own finger after and that is how she recognized its texture and sweetness.

Oh how she was maddened to attempt his entry. He sat on his haunches and she widened her legs as she stood. Amazingly, his prod was so long that she only had to slide down on its distal portion. He did not have to shift position at all. Her fears dissipated without difficulty. Her tunnel took all of him and expanded with his cocks seemingly infinite reaching into her. She herself growled mightily at their perfect interlocking. The growl echoed away as her moans succeeded them.

Her being was so deliciously speared as she squatted to his base and then rose back to his cock's full height. She threw her head back and cupped her low slung, pendulous yet so firm mounds. Then she lifted one to her mouth and sucked greedily on its tender midnight tip. She rhythmically squeezed the other.

She was converting into a piston on his joint as she pounded her insides against him.

He must have relished her riding him in any manner she conceived as he extended into her more deeply with each passing second.

And now her legs vibrated like an archers spent bowstring. Her energy was merging into her lower body and it was building frightfully and would not be diverted. A howl, short and sharp, escaped Vincent as he poured his shiny white substance into her. Every spasm of his brought further consolidation for her, an ecstatic coalescence of engulfing hot power to her center. The first exploding wave of her release made her groan and shake. Each subsequent wave was greater until she was awash in delirious pleasure.

The peak then subsided and she and Vincent slackened and were drained.

This was only a beginning for them.

Chapter 36

Witches Brew

The suggestion was seemly to Danika; it would be a witch's brew to all others she was certain. She had not verbalized it but would do so within the next twenty four hours.

Henry and Adelaide's estate was too apparent a haven. Danika did not have the absolute influence over the children here that she had in her rocky lair. Her particular certainty was that she would return them there. She and Hansel and Gretel had to be in flight again shortly. This had been but a momentary refuge for the children to recover while Danika endeavored to persuade the children to grant her transforming them into her kind.

Firstly, she was not compelled to reveal her plans to Henry and Adelaide. She respected them highly as empathetic human beings who had an absolute right to be informed of Hansel and Gretel's whereabouts and wellbeing; Juria less so as she was not particularly attached to him anymore. She had supposed their love would never perish. She had written that to him as a younger woman and ecstatic bride. She had been sorely wrong. Changes had stamped themselves upon her indelibly.

Secondly, Danika wished for companionship in her marvelous, albeit lonely, undead existence. Who better to share adventures with forever than with her own children? As any vampire was capable, she could have already created miniature replicas of herself. She had to have Hansel and Gretel's consent however. She cherished them and was not willing to subject them to an eternity that was not of their selection. On that point, she felt absolute, she thought?

She had many convincing arguments for why the undead life was beautiful beyond a mortal's comprehension. She regretted nothing, savored everything once having decided upon her inhuman path. Her love for Juria had been dashed when he had not been brave enough to have paired with her in this experiment. Had he dedicated himself to this forever opportunity as she had, the entire family would, without question, be undead. Damn his obstinacy she thought!

And she had not killed Juria and absconded with her son and daughter then as she preferred Hansel and Gretel to age a bit prior to removing them from Juria and Claire's not altogether unappreciated care of them.

Critically also, half of every day she had to spirit herself away to a casket, cave or other chambers and containers impervious to natural sunlight. The two infants would have perished under those conditions.

Again and again, Danika also refused to turn them involuntarily. These were her children! As their Mother, she was obligated and determined to provide them with quality options. But these options had to be selected by them. And so the children had to be capable of speech and higher thought before genuine answers could be given. Therefore, they remained with their Father and Stepmother.

Her hunger subsided as her feeding had been sufficient. She had absentmindedly pushed the cadaver away after avidly slurping the last ounce of blood from his gaping wound into her own system. Fanglike teeth sparkled through the ooze. Automatically, she backhandedly wiped the crimson red drool from her mouth corners.

The victim splayed at her feet with legs akimbo and head at right angle to his chest was a gruesome sight. Danika even recoiled and winced moderately but just for a moment. She must tidy this up. She leaned to the cobblestone street and placed the head in its proper alignment. She ignored the legs as they were too cumbersome; sufficient that she mused.

She mutated and took to the air, beating at its currents powerfully. Her destination was back to the estate.

She hoped that Henry had tended to her needs for a dirt bed. What a quaint thought dirt bed was. She was drunk with fluid and chortled, as much as a bat can do so, at the image. She was actually very fond of the smell and feel of soil upon her backside as she was held rigid within her confines. A dirt bed was her salvation: others might flinch, she did not care.

Once landed and dazzlingly human again, she softened. It was not wise to be savage in front of anyone. Soft played to her advantage. She manipulated people without obvious aggression. It was slick and to her liking. Yet savage was inherent in her and would always be. That harsh, violent quality was to be accepted in accompaniment with the gift of longevity.

Queen of the Damned she had been called. With her analytic mind, Philosopher Queen of the Damned was more like it. She approved of that title.

The private guesthouse yielded to space, comfort and elegance. It was the little twin brother to the manor house. It was baroque, not overly ornate and furnished for relaxation.

The wine cellar was situated in this structure. The wine cellar's unfinished foyer completed the basement portion here. As Danika passed through the upstairs, she realized that Henry had not finalized his task for her. That was so much the better as they had to talk.

The two lanterns illumined the dank walls for Henry. Her vision was a matter of pride for her as she discerned all in the pitch dark; gifts galore as a vampire. She descended the staircase. It may have led to earthen walls and floor but was itself ruggedly built for substantial traffic as wine was most likely imbibed often. Henry would have to formulate an excuse to guests and staff as he fetched all wine while she resided there.

Henry was filling the fragrant smelling wood box with shovels of soil which he had transported in buckets; the soil scooped generously from rough patches in the cemetery. He labored profusely.

His tension, she intuited, came from, not only the labor, but his effort to surround the job with silence. His every motion had to be calculated and measured. To be discovered willingly housing a vampire would cost him everything. He risked all for the true Mother of his Step grandchildren. He was a very worthy man she believed.

"Henry, thank you. Your efforts are much valued.

We have to converse, just you and me. I can trust you. I comprehend and witness that. So you must be apprised of my plans for Hansel and Gretel. Only confide in Adelaide in time. Your shock at this will fade and it is the right plan for the children. As their Mother, they will remain in my possession, not Juria's. You and I both have formed the same opinion of Juria. He does not have the sense or skills to raise them adequately even with Claire's assist."

Henry did not act as if he heard her except to nod his head in the affirmative. He mechanically persisted in stuffing the box.

"I can only have them by my side if they too are vampires. In that manner, they will rest when I rest, awaken when I awaken. But mainly I desire that they freely choose this. It would be travesty of me, it seems, to make that determination for them. Do you understand me?"

As if an automaton, Henry kept nodding in acceptance of her words. That she only glimpsed the back of his head as he did this did not alter the fact of his acceptance.

"I will have persuaded them by the next setting sun. They adore their Mother and will forever be mine.

But I will seek you and Adelaide out periodically and over and over after our exit. You will know their joy and whereabouts until the day that you die."

He spun on both feet then. Tears poured from him. He sobbed without concern for quiet, "Bless you, and bless you for that!"

She discerned that he was pathetic but pure as well at this moment.

Chapter 37

Frankness of Youth

Adelaide shut their bedroom door with precise care. The children stayed in place with eyes tightly closed waiting to hear evanescent footfalls.

Once securely alone, Hansel shuffled his position so that he crossed his arms behind his head, contemplated the ceiling beams and then spoke; conscious that Gretel was able to catch each and every word of his regardless of where he aimed his mouth.

"Gretel, I hope that you feel as I feel. When Mama first appeared to us, I was overjoyed! She's alive, I told myself. I couldn't have been happier!"

"Me too, Hansel. Our family was together again."

"Exactly! Mama and Papa were going to start again. So could we. No more misery because of Mama's death. I cried to myself I was so pleased. But . . ."

Gretel interrupted him. "Hansel, when she told us why she was alive, I got scared."

"She isn't really alive Gretel. She is undead, a vampire. She wishes that for us too."

Gretel sniffled softly. Hansel rolled in bed to glance at her.

Her obvious fright, the tears barely restrained, forced Hansel to her bedside. "Little sister, I love you and will always take care of you. I am your brother and will fight for you, and me, never-ending. So don't cry, please don't cry!"

He put his arm around her down covered shoulders. She whimpered, "I don't want to be a vampire, Hansel. Do we have to be vampires and live in cold caves or stupid pine boxes?"

Hansel laughed openly at her response. "You are a little love. And, of course, we don't have to live dreadfully like that. I love Mama. You know that. You love her too. I know that. But I don't know why she chose to live as she does. She can't change it now anyhow. And she does not like Claire or Papa much either."

"Claire is so kind and good to us, Hansel. Can they both be our Mama?"

"I am sorry sweet innocent sister but don't you notice how Mama talks about Claire? I am young still but I can figure out when someone barely tolerates someone else. Mama does not intend for Claire to be our Mother. Mama does not even intend for Papa to join us!"

"That cannot be. Mama loves Papa . . . . doesn't she?"

"I don't believe that she does anymore. She talks meanly about him. She tries not to but it slips out often. She still loves us though. But I don't ever wish to be a vampire. Mama can come visit us while we live in the cottage with Claire and Papa."

He smiled pleasantly at this image.

Then he frowned again. "Mama needs us with her though. She doesn't fancy just coming to visit. She will have us leave here."

"No, no, I won't go, Hansel! I will hide forever before I let Mama take me somewhere else. I won't leave Grandmama or Grandpapa either!"

She folded her arms in defiance while lying there.

"Hush now Gretel. We will stay with Claire and Papa. Mama will just have to understand!" His tone brooked no arguing.

"Do you believe that she will? Oh I hope so!"

Hansel doubted that their Mother would really understand. He stood by the idea that Danika, ultimately, would require her way and would do everything she could to see that her way happened. He was not about to reveal that to Gretel though. He had to shield her from the severest of potential facts about Danika. To Hansel, Danika seemed like Danika often; not his Mama but rather a stranger he was unsure of.

Each passing hour raised his level of discomfort with her. And it was not exclusively because she was a vampire. He had suspected Viktoria of being a vampire as he had heard her climb down stairs and then had heard a lid slam just before total fatigue had rendered him helpless in Viktoria's home. In that short burst of connection though, she had given off the scent of an unselfish individual. She had aided them when it was dire. She worked for their welfare during those moments. He hated this sense of alarm but it seemed that his Mama gave off the exact opposite scent and that was the scent of selfishness. Not so blatant that it was easily read but it was distinct and potent to her Son. Could she overcome this characteristic? He really didn't know.

He was frustrated, thoroughly frustrated. All that he desired out of his life were a few clear-cut, straightforward answers. Weren't there any?

Hansel and Gretel froze. A commotion was developing downstairs. They both charged from the room and ran for the bannister.

Chapter 38

Buds Blooming

Entranced yet stunned, riveted yet flabbergasted, Claire did not retreat from the scene.

Viktoria's raucous display of impulse and ache did not surprise Claire either. Viktoria did not curb her impulses when it revolved around sexual appetite.

She could be very restrained and contained when focused.

She had no focus except for release when she chose to couple. Vincent, once targeted, abrogated all selection in the matter. And so he yielded to her aggressively sensual approaches and devices without hesitation.

Apparently, Claire smirked, Vincent had managed a bit of pleasure in the encounter as his enormously extended and erupting cock had shown itself satisfied.

She speculated for the sheerest second, his size while in human form. No matter as the thought went fleeting and she found that she was content to never find out.

Temptations would come and go but Juria was forever. That was her longing since the ménage. She was certain of his identical passion. That was to be cemented by their advances once they had Hansel and Gretel safely in hand.

Claire led on once Vincent and Viktoria's fascinating antics were past. She shrugged her shoulders at Viktoria's deep-seated and compulsive erotic yearnings. If Viktoria did not restrain herself, no one else could restrain her either.

The full moon gave a telltale hint to the trails transition into road. As they surged upward along the irregular road, the tall pines transitioned into formations of slender deciduous groves, then to scrub and finally to dusty plant-less terrain.

The uniformity of green growth would abruptly rise up as they neared the estate.

Her family had transformed the area from one of high desert plateau into a thriving fertile self-sustaining community. An underground spring had been tapped long before her father and mother had taken over. The establishment of the estate would have been unthinkable were it not for the water that welled up in more than abundant supply.

If Hansel and Gretel were not with Henry and Adelaide, what then she shuddered to herself?

They must be there.

Claire did not even consider the possibility of her Stepchildren's demise. She was strong and courageous but she would not plumb those grim and ugly depths. Quite truthfully, her survival depended upon rescuing the children. Were she and Juria not able to retrieve them whole and healthy, she and her husband would be sick at heart, longtime sorrowful, maybe sustained by the other, maybe not.

Vincent loped ahead of her. Claire spurred herself on to attempt to keep up with him and to more rapidly close upon the beckoning courtyard. Juria paced alongside her. Viktoria strode next to her on the opposite side from Juria.

Viktoria leaned towards her a fraction.

"I do not wish to scare your mother and father, Claire. I could easily precede you to their door but I believe it best that they receive only you and Juria there. I will gather Vincent to me and we two will observe from a small distance."

With that said, Viktoria gracefully shot forward to the werewolf. She butted his shoulder with her shoulder and forced him to veer off from the track that Claire and Juria clung to.

The road did become more of a rutted track as the multi flowered garden and the majestic courtyard crept into Claire's sight. Those blooms were her mother's tender masterpiece. Her buds were her treasure and Claire rejoiced in that for Adelaide.

Her mother was so gently spirited in regards to her domain.

Claire further realized that Adelaide did not even conceive of it as her domain, rather as her oasis which she shared with all decent souls.

Claire was attached to her mother in a manner that was positive, spiritual and empathic. They were capable, almost, of foretelling one another's actions and agree whole heartedly with each other in these actions; except where her father was involved.

Claire sometimes hated that one element in her mother; that willingness by Adelaide of suspending all reasonable judgment and intentions in order to give help and succor to her husband. And that was yet when he was ruthlessly wrong or profoundly bigoted.

There was slight activity ahead from other than any member of her own party.

The murky black curled around everything but she was still able to faintly see and sense two individuals at the guesthouse entrance. They appeared in concentrated discussion and a jumble of scrambled and fragmented words floated to Claire's ears.

Definitely, the tones included the low pitch of a masculine voice. She guessed that as the voice of her father.

As Claire neared and Juria trailed, Claire did recognize it as Henry's speech. The alternating splashes of sound were softer, sweeter; feminine and possibly her Mother.

Claire hurried over to the figures in the dank dark. "Father, Papa, is that you? Mother, too?"

The startled figures spun to confront the oncoming voice.

Claire raced into her father's outstretched arms as he identified who she was.

She did not miss his quick glare at Juria as he also approached.

Claire had no idea who the woman was or why they were in intense very hushed discussion this late.

Well, she surmised, if I can be roused and wandering the surrounds at this twilight hour, others can be awake too!

Henry kissed Claire softly and then gently hissed a snarled "hello" at Juria. Claire suspected that Juria had flinched at this greeting by Henry.

Then Juria behaved so oddly that Claire was not adept enough to fathom it.

He clutched his chest and gasped for air as he peered at the young woman. She then heard Juria gargle out the words, "Oh my God!"

From the ruefully smiling mouth of the other woman came a reply. "Yes Juria, I exist still. I am no longer your lost wife or deceased partner.

Hansel and Gretel are safe as well."

Claire's head snapped to.

Her heart battered her chest simultaneously.

This voice, this person, this creature was no longer a part of a frozen past but was a vivid and very unpleasant portion of her present and future. Her acute sense of foreboding, in spite of the children's momentary safety, swamped her senses wholly. She shuddered with shock and anxiety.

Chapter 39

Heart Proffered

The Werewolf, Vincent, sauntered along the trail with the trio. He was capable of only a middling swiftness with middling force.

He was panting he was so drained. Had he the opportunity to lie his immense body down with head on forepaw's like a bone weary dog, he would; instantly. The lovely she-creature had sapped him of all brute strength.

His cock was softly repositioned inside his sheath with only the least of pulse affecting his spent organ.

Her writhing upon his shaft earlier remained etched into his synapses. He had refrained as she had approached and had assaulted his senses; but his primitive wolfish member had ignored all rational messages and had hued to its own mindless expansion.

She overwhelmed him so nonchalantly. She had desired him, she had taken him. It was nothing complex, simply a bolt of desire on Viktoria's part.

Her core had produced in him not only his seriously turgid tool but she had left an ember of herself inside him that was destined to endure, crackling in its bond to her. It was then that he had committed himself to her. As animal or man, she stood the largest in the warm chambers of his heart.

He padded alongside Claire as he engaged with his tidal sentiments for Viktoria.

Jeffrey Underwood

In spite of his new alliance, he was also not quitting his responsibilities to Claire. He was a captive to this obligation because he was beholden to Henry, but equally, cherished Claire in her own right. He was dedicated to deflecting harm away from her.

In and out so directly that he was hardly pricked by the thought at all was a niggling concern regarding his tie to Claire. What if Claire and Viktoria ever clashed? What then?

He shook his bestial head, gnashed his teeth and tossed that notion into the void of the heavens. It was not about to ever happen so he gave that consideration short shrift.

He was convinced that, once sexually joined, Viktoria absolutely realized that his heart was offered to her.

She had touched him lightly as the estate grew closer. The style of touch was that of honeyed affection, freshly roused heartfelt connection and soft massaging strokes meant to endear Vincent to her.

As canid, he displayed love and regard with nuzzling rubs from his muzzle and a responding thick cock swell. His range was extremely limited in this incarnation. What he revealed was more than clear and sufficient though.

The steady pace kept his very primitive brain motoring as best it could.

Their future interplay was to be creative for sure. She stirred from her casket just as he shed his costume of human skin. They would have to revel in the bestial, which each would offer the other.

How then to find the more sophisticated side to their rapport? Ah yes, they were to communicate in notes; notes of his outsize passion for her, notes of his ponderings and ruminations, notes of his activities as well. The written word was to be their entwined glory. He would keep her awash in poems brilliantly exposing their fused spirits or paeans dedicated to his newfound delight and joy consummated. This solution was beyond adequate, possibly sublime even.

Their success was to be the pinnacle of his lifespan. His gratitude rose up his vigor and he was electric with it.

Viktoria shouldered him into the feeble brush and separated them from Claire and Juria.

He automatically recovered his present orientation, gauged Claire and Juria to be behind and the estate courtyard to be in front.

He avidly paired with Viktoria as they took themselves from any natural line of sight. He tailed Viktoria.

They were to hide in the dimness, observe and suspend involvement until their assistance might be required. After all, if Hansel and Gretel were inside the estate, so might be the kidnapper.

No need to reveal all strength and numbers immediately. Claire and Juria were first; he and Viktoria next if needed.

It was then that Vincent recognized the presence of a man and a woman in resolute conversation at the entrance to one of the larger abodes. Viktoria tensed abruptly and he knew that she was aware of the same.

To herself, Viktoria susurrated, "What keeps her from me and me from her? She shields herself yet. Can she visualize me? Well, apparently she cannot. She must be too distracted to do so."

Vincent was unable to make sense of these hushed musings. He dismissed them in his trust of Viktoria. If she uttered them then the words were meaningful. Let her put all that she believed essential together. He was not about to interrupt or disturb her in any capacity.

After several minutes, Claire, Juria, Henry and the unknown female silenced one another as they walked awkwardly to the manor house.

Juria appeared ready to swoon and collapse, Claire and he had extended arms around waists for support, Henry paced stridently toward the broad door of the imposing primary abode and the auburn tressed, shapely beauty propelled herself with a satisfied air of lightness.

This scene in motion had to be watched closely and vigilantly. An explosion of emotions was soon occurring. The atmosphere enveloping these four was supercharged and heavy.

He and Viktoria hunched more so. Viktoria's sibilant growl seeped out in almost suppressed tones as the mysterious woman's presence closed distance and then passed by. They were not detected.

Though it seemed that Viktoria would have cared naught; it was obvious to Vincent that Viktoria barely stifled and restrained herself.

Once the oaken entrance door swung shut without a sound, werewolf and vampire smoothly located themselves beneath locked but bright windows. Their hearing pierced the wall and glass as butter yielding to the cold and merciless knife edge.

Interior voices elevated, commotion developed.

Vincent and Viktoria tensed at the same instant. They equally knew that a tempest of marathon magnitudes was about to engulf them. Sheer survival in a contest of strength and wills was looming; this storm was so ready to boom its presence for all to see and hear.

Even Vincent felt terror bolt through him.

Viktoria appeared to remain taut but composed and set for any event. He admired her confidence. She had nerves of hard, cold steel.

Chapter 40

Grand to Grim

His unconscious blossomed into a rotting fetid remembrance of Danika's magnetic interest in ceaseless life. He and she had toyed with the prospects of vampirism often in the formative stages of their marriage. He had let this fantastical game of theirs drift and bob eventually from his perception; it became a mental remnant that disappeared entirely.

And he had believed the same of Danika as it had vanished as discussion between them. His naiveté had fooled him harshly he saw.

His knees weakened to the point of being unstable. His head had been crushed in wave after wave of sheer incredulity. His happiness that she remained animate was completely blanketed by his shock, shame and dismay that he had been indubitably deceived; deceived and now in despair having instantaneously realized that she had abandoned him and their children for her selfish pursuit. Prior grand love for Danika was irrevocably broken; grim in the starkness of that disappearance.

He and the children had been betrayed so that she could pursue fangs and blood, years without end, power vainglorious.

Her ravishing looks were a cruel façade; to him, she just as well was a smiling, hateful skull with a cloak of beautiful skin. As Claire boosted him up, Juria shrank from the revealed Danika. This vampire parading as a person, he was convinced, had no genuine heart for others.

His despair and loathing was only held at bay by Claire at his side and the sense that he was about to be shown Hansel and Gretel, breathing and presumably well.

He did not grow literally sick only because he had nothing in his stomach to churn upward. Brutal hunger had few niceties but that was one.

He lurched to maintain a pace with the others. He mustered a thankful glance at Claire for her efforts to stand him tall. When he quickly peered at Claire, he turned concerned for her. She had no more food in her belly than did he. And now she was pallid enough to contrast highly with the inked black night. She was in profound silent shock.

They both had to sit before they dropped to the soil underneath their feet. The door was their reprieve. Henry flung it open fully and, as they all entered, remembered himself and closed it such that it would not be heard shutting.

Juria and Claire dragged each other over to the breakfast nook. Henry roughly pulled out chairs for them. Danika did not sit, instead lingered in a random corner.

Juria barked with all his remaining fortitude, "Where are my children!? Danika has not harmed them, has she? And your wife, sir, where is Adelaide?"

Danika snarled at that. "I would never mistreat them, you misbegotten soul. I am their Mother, fool!"

Danika paused. Juria grasped that she was endeavoring to rein in her anger at him.

Within her pause, footfalls thudded from the ceiling above and then Hansel and Gretel, wide eyed in their confusion yet delirious in their pleasure that Juria and Claire were both present, both safe, dashed to them.

The adorable rascals flung themselves down the stairwell, rode the banister and popped into their Father and Stepmother's awaiting and extended arms. Adelaide was on their heels, gleeful at her daughter and son in law's unexpected arrival.

Simultaneously, tears leaked from his and Claire's reddened, wearied eyes.

Finally, after so much anxious anguish and strained torment, the family of four was reunited. It seemed an eternity since the children had been placed in bed at the cottage, ostensibly secure then and sleeping soundly.

Danika was forgotten in the exuberant moment. Everything in Juria's soul belonged to Hansel and Gretel. He was determined to be the finest of fathers going forward.

Gretel sang out, "Papa, Mama, stay always with Hansel and me!"

Hansel sobbed, "We don't want to be separated from you ever again!"

Juria's intuition envisioned Danika's revulsion at the endearing scene she was forced to watch. He intuited also that Henry stepped closer to Danika.

Adelaide's kisses poured onto Juria's head, then Claire's, on to Hansel and Gretel's.

From her corner, Danika spoke with quiet menace and unvarnished disdain, "They belong to me, Juria. That Gretel calls Claire 'Mama' is disgusting. I will have the children as a genuine mother is entitled. You were their short-term caretaker, you and Claire. You two were nothing more than that. Now that your Father realizes that you are uninjured, you, Hansel and Gretel, will come with me.

Juria, you may thank me for that courtesy sometime in the future. That is if I ever opt to have them see you again. I will however, make an exception for Henry and Adelaide in this regard as they have been very good to me."

Juria only retched up empty air again at this arrogant insult of hers.

Henry shot a scowl at Juria as Juria spun to confront Danika.

His retching had subsided.

Henry proclaimed, "Hansel, Gretel, do as your Mother says! Now! Claire, Adelaide, cease any resistance! I command you both!"

The children whimpered, "No, no." But they prepared to do as their Mama and Grandpapa demanded.

Adelaide bowed her head and spoke to Hansel and Gretel, "Your Mama recognizes what is best for you. And were we to resist Danika anyhow, she will simply take you. Henry and I have to support her greater strength here . . . . sadly.

And, she is your Mother, after all. There is no other choice. Take my hands now." They walked slowly to where Danika and Henry remained.

Danika raised her voice as Juria advanced upon her. "I wish that the children be turned. I have waited years for this opportunity. They continue to say no and I say yes. My patience at their young mind's resistance has vanished. If I am honest with myself, I gave them latitude to agree in my surety that they would be convinced to be with me. I use force only in necessity or as a last resort. But I have seen their hesitancy and, as their Mother, I have resolved that I, as Adelaide pointed out, know the soundest alternatives for them.

And it is time to make the decision! I have waited years for this after all. We three will travel the world as undead. None of you has the might to stop me. I do not desire leaving anyone's blood here but will if blocked. Approach me no further."

Juria raged at her unholy strength. He was helpless in the face of it. Claire braced at Juria's hip. He comprehended that she would wait for his next action.

Chapter 41

Hatred Unleashed

Dirt was laid neatly half way up the sides of the plain rectangular pine box.

Henry was extremely precise and Danika had asked him to not pile it too high.

He abided by that as his entire scheme was to placate Danika at all costs. All involved, knowingly or not, were at her behest. The force of the vampire seethed with continuously at-the-ready fury. This capability made her omnipotent to him.

Her weaknesses were occasional and unlikely; her strengths were legion beyond imagining.

She was generous enough to deal with Adelaide and him involving the children; involving anything actually. She, were she so inclined, could feed upon him as her whim directed.

All in him abandoned any possibility of overpowering her. She may have been slave to feeding as time slipped away at length but, also, she could kill without any reason whatsoever even when not hungry. There was that and that was dangerous enough. He did not wish the death of his wife or himself.

Danika was fully able to procure Hansel and Gretel without a backward glimpse or a shred of doubt or hesitation. Hers was the power, the glory, forever. She gave the impression of being a god in the range of her capacities.

He had to be visited by his Step grandchildren in his and Adelaide's twilight years. He cherished them as did Adelaide. Without them, their ebbing years were to be bleak and empty.

Wealth was no healer unless those advantages could be shared with kith, kin and dear others.

Claire was kin of course but he despised her husband. To witness her with him was greater than emptiness. For Henry, it went to a place within him that screamed agony and torture! Juria was so unworthy of his daughter! How could she have done this to him!

When finished, he and Danika drifted upstairs, then outside. Henry queried her, "What did you find so attractive about Juria that you married him? Pray tell, how did that happen?"

As Danika spilled out her theories, very commonplace theories as her descriptions colored them, of just what her attachment to Juria consisted of, Henry evaluated Danika's appearance.

Her capacities as one of the undead appealed to him thoroughly. Her perfection in line and shape closed the book for him ultimately. He was smitten and he was aroused. She struck a divine chord with his baser instincts.

There was not an intellectual particle that tugged him to her. Yes, she was articulate. Yes, she was swift and keen of mind.

But no, that mattered little to Henry. By far, it was her flowing grace and superlative exterior that drove its spike into him. She did not wear extraordinary raiment yet that fueled the effect. She was in plain clothing and she still expressed a lush and tawny splendor.

Her hair alone made his inhalations catch often. The definite auburn mane was thick with abundant natural curls and had a rich luster that was really quite divine.

The bounteous hair framed a face of high set, delicate angles with apple tinted creamy soft skin. No lines were remotely noticeable. Her light emerald orbs glistened and flashed. What a wonderfully smooth, regal, gently arched throat she revealed as she bore down upon him with her thoughts.

He understood there was an underlying intensity to her being. That compressed energy wove through her speech, her movements, even her still posture.

The arousal manifested itself in him as he feigned shyness, lowered his eyes and filled them with her form below her chin and throat.

She and Adelaide in her youth struck similar images; proud, heavy breasts, flared hips at narrowed waist, very trim buttocks, legs of gorgeous length and tapir. Granted, a bit of this was imagined as he was not privy to discerning all the details of her shape hidden by her garb but he was of little doubt that he was keenly accurate.

They were interrupted abruptly by Claire's voice.

It was muffled to begin and so he was uncertain of its possessor. Then she broke through the sheets of dark and he glimpsed her. It was his dearest Claire. They embraced.

He peered over her shoulder and, as he expected, Juria's countenance became identifiable. Henry flinched and frowned. His "hello" was short, clipped, and sour.

Henry observed Juria as Juria recognized Danika for the first time and, as Henry anticipated, the weakling nearly collapsed in front of Danika and him.

Claire hurriedly released herself from her Father and leaped to her Husband.

Henry hushed them all and led the way to the manor house.

Danika, not Claire, was now his pride. He had allied himself entirely with the ethereal vampire. That would be proved by his actions once ensconced within the walls of the structure towering above them.

Having settled in the side room off the kitchen, Henry planned on being the first to address the group. He was not first though.

He was caught off-guard and was momentarily flummoxed when Juria bellowed out at Danika and him. Juria had audacious nerve to shout at Henry in Henry's own house.

Danika tossed her insult into the taut hollow of the room. Henry had been prepared to toss Juria from his presence then but was halted by Hansel and Gretel's tumultuous entrance into the room so he merely sidled up to Danika instead. He was letting it be known by this repositioning of his that he would brook no disagreement with Danika or himself.

He crossed his arms over his chest and cocked a stern, lashing glower toward the enmeshed and glad individuals at the table, including Adelaide.

Danika sheered through the celebration with a sharp and pointed declaration. Henry seconded this declaration with a clear, definitive command. And with that, Adelaide complied and escorted Hansel and Gretel over to their Mother.

The children's tears elicited no empathy from him. This was occurring for their benefit he believed . . . and his and Adelaide's too, of course.

Danika was resolute. So was Henry. It mattered not as Juria came for Danika and the children. Henry smirked as Danika stopped Juria abruptly with a warning. Henry liked that; it pleased him no end.

His hatred had been unleashed. Woe to those who obstructed Danika and him. He would kill Juria himself were Claire's husband to take another pace nearer. He would take Juria down in front of his own daughter if necessary.

This righteous anger felt so appropriate to Henry.

Chapter 42

Dutifully Done

Adelaide was ever so weary.

Hansel and Gretel were tucked tightly into their beds and she had seen them to thick sleep whilst humming mellifluous and melodic sweet lullabies. It was soothing even for her. This was how it should be: her loved ones secure in the manor's embrace, drowsing comfortably and rapidly to the syncopation of their Grandmama's voice, the surroundings peaceful, still, harmonious.

She sensed that this tranquility was not to last. Harboring a vampire, mother or no, was unsettling to Adelaide. That Henry was drawing dirt for Danika's coffin at this very moment disturbed her no end. There seemed much unpredictability coiled in the atmosphere, ready to assert itself and be launched forcefully.

That was why the weariness; no matter her efforts, disturbance and discord were preeminent and imminent.

On schedule, the rapid patter of feet charged in opposite direction from the gently tiptoeing Adelaide. She whirled in time to witness a flash of Gretel's nightgown concealed bottom. Hansel was already around the corner and descending the stairs.

Adelaide hastened to narrow the gap between them. She had heard discussion downstairs just before the children had exploded out of their room. She recognized it as vigorous speech, sharp retorts too. Tranquility had had its way and was past.

Adelaide basically tripped into the group hug that was still ensuing with Juria, Claire, Hansel and Gretel. It was beyond delight, if she had to stumble, to have stumbled into those particular arms.

They caught her easily and righted her quickly. She instantly pressed kisses to each and every available head. She was so emotional that she paid no attention to Danika or Henry's absence from the embrace whatsoever.

As a matter of fact, comprehending her husband's antipathy for Juria, she sincerely hoped for his silence so that the magical spell between the five of them would last infinitely. Please Henry, she pleadingly cogitated, do not spoil this!

The revelry was crushed then but not by Henry. Adelaide was surprised as she heard Danika, with vampire lip tightly curled, spew out intense sentiment regarding possession of Hansel and Gretel.

Adelaide had to decide shortly to who her alliance would be.

She wavered only until Henry ordered the children into action. She had to assist the frightened two. So, as a reflex also, she took their hands softly, expressed words to them that she was hardly aware of and then guided them over to their Mother.

And, after all, Danika was truly their Mother. Who was she, Adelaide? Not blood; only a sensitive and gentle woman who loved Hansel and Gretel so. She had no genuine right to keep them from Danika.

Henry sought it as well. So the deed was dutifully done.

A gorge formed as her throat became inflamed and then tightened simultaneously.

She felt ripped open and close to disintegration into bits and pieces of her present disparate self. If she had revealed her genuine being, the lamentations would have been heard worldwide. She, though, had to pretend that all was as it should be.

Sharing Hansel and Gretel gracefully was at the core of Adelaide's yearnings.

The heavy reality was that an adversarial situation was developing and she was its slave rather than its master.

So, then, she released her pain and permitted it to descend into some chasm of hers that felt bottomless and thereby endurable. It was not without end though and was also not tolerable. It purely let her function automatically, briefly, in anesthetized motion and thought.

She was situated at Henry's side, trembling only minutely.

The five of them now faced Juria and Claire, her treasured daughter.

The misery upon her daughter's visage was awful to behold. That misery was in the process of shrinking and pinching all that had been a sight extraordinaire.

And Juria, his ragged rage was scarcely contained. His teeth clenched so intensively that Adelaide felt his jaws must fracture. He had been betrayed by Danika not once but twice; the marriage abandonment then and the family takeover now.

And Henry had permitted his unholy biases to do the same to Juria; Henry's treachery was intolerable too.

And then there was Adelaide. She stiffly shuffled before them. She might have been the worst she sensed, paralyzed, as she tacitly let this event proceed.

Danika dragged Hansel and Gretel to the oaken door separating indoors from outdoors. Claire dropped to her knees and shrieked, "My God, no!"

Juria rushed up to Henry, slapped him with resounding sound and force, stared wildly at Adelaide and then Claire. Then he gave chase to Danika.

Henry pursued Juria in anger and with all attention toward slowing Juria, insuring Danika's escape.

Adelaide observed all this, grasped all this in a blink.

She ran to embrace her tearful, sobbing daughter. Claire had to be resurrected somehow. Adelaide was determined to be the means by which Claire was to recover. But Claire pushed her Mother away. "How could you?" Claire panted out.

Adelaide was devastated. How was it that the pain intensified and did not cease intensifying? "Please my daughter, I am sorry beyond what you can imagine. I am a foolish, foolish old woman!"

Claire continued to weep.

Even as her grief engulfed her, Adelaide heard the huge main door slam violently. After that, all of her attention returned to this room and her inconsolable daughter.

Gaping wounds were pouring forth an ocean full of pain and suffering for most all; the two in this room for sure!

Adelaide was fully willing to make a pact with the devil to secure harmony for her loved ones. In her core, she knew that she already had formulated that pact with Henry; and harmony was not to be the outcome for those involved. Could her devil be forgiven? Could she be forgiven?

Chapter 43

Harsh Desserts

Day was commencing to close in upon them and Viktoria was desperate to take action. A wicked grin sliced through her features of a sudden.

She signaled Vincent to remain in place.

Initially, she concocted a method to possibly neutralize Danika. It was too late though to discover a Hawthorne grove and retrieve a branch to use as a pinion; her streaking velocity still was not enough for that as she was uncertain of locating such trees.

She would have to leave the plateau at a minimum.

Ah, she considered, here is the way! That generated the grin and then she vanished. She had not chosen to waste seconds reforming herself. She dashed as only a vampire can.

Upon her return, she discerned Vincent's amazement at her efficiency and strength. She was back in minutes.

What truly dumbfounded Vincent, Viktoria was able to plainly observe via wolfish pupil dilation, was that she clutched such a large, dense limb. The limb dwarfed her hands as she positioned it horizontally across her chest. One end was thinner and useless. The other end was the critical portion. She had split it from the trunk and wood had sheered with splinters flying. A gaping hole was left behind in the tree.

The area where she had rent the limb was torn at an acute angle, forming a deadly long edged apex with support to match. She deemed it to be quite a wonderful makeshift weapon; more than adequate for the purpose. It also gave her confidence to spring when necessary.

Necessity leapt at her without hesitation; and she leapt back.

The massive manor door burst outward as it moaned and then cracked against the proximate wall. To the uninformed and slumbering staff it was as if a canon had been ignited.

Danika, Hansel and Gretel shot from the egress and tore into the shadows.

Viktoria thrust herself at Danika before Danika converted to winged form and flew with the young ones in her clutches. Danika must not be allowed to elevate them where, in the imminent melee, they could plunge downward and die.

Just prior to contact, Viktoria's inner vision revealed to her that Danika heard her harsh rush of sound, that she comprehended the furious massed being charging and that she readied all of her defenses. Viktoria exploded upon her just as Danika flung Hansel and Gretel away to each side of her.

Viktoria swung the timber at Danika's skull. Inner vision obviously returned to Danika and she lowered her head and shifted around to confront the 'assaulter. Viktoria's weapon was inadvertently tossed out of Viktoria's hands and reach when her arms wildly arched and upon striking emptiness was unable to continue clasping it.

Viktoria's balance teetered and she gasped as Danika took the transitory opportunity to extend her upper extremities with their blood red pointed nails at Viktoria's heart. If she were to pierce to and through Viktoria's heart, Viktoria would be critically debilitated at the very outset; not annihilated or thoroughly vanquished instantly but certainly soon to be. Being weakened such, Danika would plunge the very stake into her own heart that had been intended for Danika's heart.

Viktoria's immortality wavered as Danika thrust gleaming nails through her thin and worthless gown.

As her blood welled up and out of the wounds below left breast and nipple, as Danika gleefully forced her digits deeper, Vincent hurtled himself at Danika with shrieking howls and grotesque snarls. He crashed into Danika with a tidal strength that even Danika was incapable of resisting.

Danika collapsed into the hard compressed earth under his ferocity just long enough for Viktoria to pull away from those deadly nails. She regained her balance and she too heaved herself maximally back upon Danika.

Viktoria's now powerful psychic vision informed her that Henry and Juria froze in horror at the scene before them. Both raced to Hansel and Gretel, Henry hoisted Gretel and Juria the same for Hansel. Then the men spun on their heels and returned them to the distraught women inside. Those women quickly gathered their composure and covered the children protectively with their bodies as if bullets and shrapnel were raining down on them.

Adelaide and Claire cooed into their ears as the young ones huddled beneath them and whimpered plaintively.

Sorrow swallowed them all.

The men pounded to the outside but then were immobilized, perplexed, and remorseful suddenly. Juria screamed, "Stop, stop! We can solve this some other way, surely! Please stop!"

Henry spoke not a word but was abashed and ashamed.

Viktoria did not wish to yield now that Vincent had added his potent might to the fray. Viktoria flexed her neck and viewed her oozing wounds and was immediately blanketed with an uncontrollable demonic fury. Danika thrashed below Vincent as Vincent pinned her soundly down with arms of unimaginably thick power.

Viktoria was galvanized as she recalled her stake. Where was it? She sprinted to it, driving the very air to part and hiss for her. Confidence blew through her as she lifted it up to her. Who cared what Juria was shouting! She thought to hell with either Henry or him; most especially, to hell with Danika. Danika would invade Viktoria's space no longer.

In seconds, she reversed and pulled Vincent off of Danika and with hard shove plunged the sharp edged limb into Danika's chest. It did not matter the precise location of the stab in relation to her heart as it was not Hawthorn. It would not kill her; simply stick her to the ground where she lay.

But Viktoria knew what was about to kill Danika. And she pulsed with orgasm at the notion.

Viktoria flung herself to the private guest house then. That visionary aspect of hers informed her of the pine box. She was safely ensconced within its confines. She was a survivor without a doubt.

Just prior to the anesthesia of undead dreams, she perceived the outcome of her pitched battle with Danika.

Luminosity crept slowly up towards the sky's ceiling. A brightening was at the brink.

Vincent remained sentry over Danika as she was pinned to the soil. She attempted to rip the wood from her chest cavity, she attempted to struggle free and fatally wound Vincent. Her efforts, even with vampirish velocity and force, were unsuccessful.

Like an arrow released, sun's rays glanced, then struck Danika directly. She was unmercifully cremated; features blackened became ashy and then she blasted into an infinite number of ashen flakes. The stake sent its heated flame up at Vincent. He staggered backward and then began his quick torture into human form.

Viktoria lost consciousness with a singular comprehension. And that was that Danika had received her just and harsh desserts.

Sad in its own way however as Danika had once been a young, romantic, idealistic and very cherished woman.

Chapter 44

Pieces In Place

"Did we cause this?" Gretel tremulously whispered. She panted out these muffled words as tears began to surge.

Hansel shivered in fright and misery as his knees quite literally knocked together. He was powerless in finding his tongue whatsoever. His characteristic maturity was just blown to bits.

The two heard Claire and Adelaide simultaneously answer. Adelaide deferred to Claire while continuing to kneel over her and her brother, stroking Gretel's hair so soothingly.

These words of Claire's calmed Gretel some, "You are loved by all and none of this is either your or Hansel's fault. It is an adult problem. Know that my little treasure . . . it is an adult problem."

"What will happen outside?" Hansel intoned as best as he could. Hansel glimpsed Adelaide and Claire peer at each other. His welling tears blurred his sight yet he perceived the fear and confusion on their faces.

Hansel precipitously shook from head to toe, sobbing, and "Someone will die out there! It was a, a, a terrible thing that was going on."

This occasion Claire and Adelaide declared in unison, "We must all stay here. This is the only safe place!"

Hansel rose up dramatically as the three men strode into their cramped space.

"What is it?" begged Hansel.

He did not recognize the third male who set himself shoulder to shoulder with his Papa and Grandpapa. It was no matter as he pitched himself into Juria's arms.

Gretel threw herself that direction too. Juria snared her as well. Both children cried their joy at Juria and Henry's survival.

Hansel scrutinized his Papa's features, especially his reddened eyes. It was then that he surmised and knew. "Mama died, didn't she?"

Gretel wept hard upon hearing Hansel's question. Surely her Mama was still alive!

Then Gretel felt Claire hug her and spotted Juria and Claire clasp hands around her. They rocked gently together. She was less upset with all of the horror once her Grandpapa, Grandmama and brother joined the group.

No one spoke through this.

Hansel finally managed, "I didn't want her to die. I didn't choose to be with her either. She was not really my Mama." His solemnity was heartbreaking.

Gretel nodded her approval. She had been terrified of the new version of Danika. Her glistening eyes locked with Claire's. "You are my Mama and always will be."

Hansel shuddered as he envisioned their future as perpetually dwarfed vampires. Growing up and becoming as his Papa and Claire were was his greatest hope. He cherished Claire and his Papa alike. Pieces for him and Gretel were tumbling into place.

Hansel was curious, though, as to who the beaming stranger was. "Papa, who is he?" Hansel extended his finger at Vincent.

Juria grinned unabashedly. "That is your Stepmother and my friend, Vincent. He is your friend also. There is another woman who came with our troop. I am sure that you remember Viktoria. The four of us aided one another for the last several days in our search for you. Their assistance has been invaluable. It was vital outside just now in addition."

Juria next chuckled. "As both you and Gretel realize, Viktoria is resting right now."

Juria swiveled his head toward Henry. "Many thanks for your having prepared that bed for Viktoria."

Hansel was uncertain the tension between the two men but it whooshed from the room after this exchange.

His Grandpapa's stance shriveled and he commented, "Anytime that I can be of service to you and Claire, I will be. You can rest assured of that."

Hansel was glad as his Papa again thanked his Grandpapa.

Chapter 45

Forgiveness Supreme

Her soul seized and the undetectable contractions generated smashing agony.

Then Henry and Juria quickly deposited the children with her and her Mother. The inner ache eased and Claire shielded Hansel and Gretel. Adelaide joined her.

The males promptly rotated out and departed. She and her Mother focused their entire effort on alleviating the terror the young ones expressed. Claire, while she also stroked their heads and cheeks, imagined the wrathful scene outdoors.

If it were Viktoria alone against Danika, what would tip the scales as these two amazingly formidable and equally capable foes assaulted one another? That the events of the last several minutes occurred as they did revealed that only Danika, Viktoria and Vincent were the engaged individuals.

Vincent was the key to Danika's demise then. She prayed that he would succeed where Viktoria alone might not. Fear gripped her foundation that Danika might prevail. That was the possible outcome which again produced sweeping dread into her.

Claire's stomach heaved momentarily; she clenched her eyes shut and kept her lips compressed together and the wave of nausea passed.

Strangely, her Mother's presence rounded the edges of her anger at her. She had been more than ready to disown both her Father and Mother as Danika absconded with Claire's son and daughter. And that was precisely her sentiments for the quaking boy and girl beneath her. It was as if they had emerged from her womb. They were infinitely valued with hearts similar to hers. She and Juria had nurtured them principally.

Danika was Mother only as blood was; otherwise, her absenteeism had been inexcusable. She, Juria, Hansel and Gretel had fused in the nurturing. And experiencing what was so unmistakably a fundamental connection between her own Mother and her Mother's Step grandchildren gave the lie to spurning her parents over this fiasco; of course, presuming the children were ultimately saved.

Henry and Adelaide had committed an egregious error but were relenting, she could see. Adelaide twined with her and Henry with Juria in this calamity. She had to forgive them. She supposed that Juria would do the same. The wound had punctured severely rendering the act of forgiveness supremely difficult. But it must be done!

Hansel reared up, inadvertently rolling Claire partially over.

Adelaide, observing Hansel, released Gretel as Gretel followed suit with her brother.

When Claire recovered, she burst toward Juria, her Father and Vincent as well with her Mother moving rapidly just behind. Vincent, the human Vincent, held a huge grin up to her. Juria simply vibrated with an aura of relief. Henry had a tear smudged visage. The battle was plainly over. The children were to remain with Juria and her.

Delirious tumult ensued and Claire rejoiced.

Juria expressed himself to her Father. Then everyone collapsed into a heap as their terror, then joy, gave way to enervation.

Upon awakening to what must have been a complete cycle of the sun, Claire was famished. Juria was a comatose lump next to her. She paused and absorbed his sweet, sweet presence. Then she gracefully withdrew from the bedroom without disturbing her dear husband.

She trundled down to the kitchen and surveyed as the manor cook staff prepared platters and platefuls of breakfast food at her Mother's direction.

Adelaide oversaw the gastronomic maneuverings with an ease born of verve, practice and skill. Claire loved her Mother. She liked her as well. Claire was then not able to suppress a long needed and long in coming smile her way.

Claire was unaware of her Father's location. Her surmise was that he was up, had eaten and was outdoors tending to, more than likely, a maintenance detail. It was laughable but he had to be involved though he had expert staff to perform these functions.

Her Father was a curmudgeon and a character but he was sensitive enough to adjust under extremes of circumstance. Her conviction was that he had been humbled to a degree; adequate for him to step back and rapidly reevaluate her and Juria's marriage and Juria himself. She was about to test her intuitions in a conversation with her Mother.

Claire sat herself at the table and attempted to delicately feast on a variety of fruits, breads, frothy milk, a large pot of porridge in addition. Claire had no restraint to begin, lost her delicacy instantaneously and devoured many of the delicious items set before her. The sweet cream and soft butter enticed her the most.

Her Mother timed her entrance properly. Claire was just sated when Adelaide slid onto a chair opposite Claire.

"My darling, how do you feel?" Adelaide gently probed.

"Mother, I deemed that we were on a precipice a day ago, you and me. I seethed in disbelief at your and Father's behavior.

Then you revealed your genuine and raw sentiments while we protected Hansel and Gretel together. My heart would not stay hard and cold then.

You are my Mother, you brought me into this world and you have foibles too. Your choices were difficult that dark early predawn and I understand. In understanding, I also forgive you, you and Father. I can sense his transformation. And he, stubborn as he can be, had further ground to makeup than you. You were ambivalent; he was strident, as usual. But I discern a softening between him and Juria. Do you notice that as well?"

Claire felt her Mother melt before her.

"He is aghast at his actions. I am aghast at my own. Thank you much for the so gracious and wished for forgiveness! You have never given such a unique and fine gift to your parents before. That you are such a caring woman, a wonderful daughter, I could not ask for more! That opinion is your father's too.

We both recognize that which we almost lost. You, Juria, Hansel and Gretel will be esteemed by us forevermore."

Claire reached across the table, clasped and squeezed her Mother's faintly quivering hands.

Some moments later, the room was crackling with activity as Hansel, Gretel and Juria had swarmed down upon the repast.

Claire asked after Viktoria and Vincent. She was informed that they had departed in the night, side by side, werewolf and vampire. Claire pondered that Vincent must have concluded she was perfectly capable of taking care of herself. Or maybe her Father had released him from his obligation. Either possibility delighted Claire as she was pleased for their mutual freedom.

It was after the banquet that she, Juria, Hansel and Gretel took their leave in order to visit, they would feel as guests initially, their home once again. The corners of Claire's lips lifted at the irony.

Chapter 46

Fully Reestablished

Juria enthusiastically chopped at the fir base. The revival of normality was a most definite blessing for all of them.

They reached the cottage a week ago and had encountered no unusual or disruptive event on their return trek. Hansel and Gretel babbled happily and attacked the cottage door upon approach.

They were in their daily classroom with their eager to learn peers and their Mother was at home. He and Claire had almost shaken the shock of the cataclysm from their skins; their bond was nearly fully reestablished.

Juria waited with swing poised at its apex. He shifted his stance then and gazed in the direction of the cottage. It was time to eliminate the last vestiges of uncertainty from that epic period. Their connection was to be fully reestablished soon. He slung his tool over his shoulder and marched home without hesitation.

Cold frost limned the edges of the structure as he crossed into the interior. His visible breath faded and he rubbed his hands together for warmth. Claire must have intuited his coming as she waited for him. He sensed her heat in her demeanor and her sheer raiment. The flames from the sizzling wood in the central hearth commingled with her heat.

Juria experienced the inevitable passion for her. She wore a linen material with a light and low bodice, sleeves tied with linen cord at mid arm. It riveted his attention upon her as she must have planned. The linen permitted him to view the outline of her lush form.

He came to her then. They kissed deeply, hungrily for the first time since the crisis began. He tasted and drank of her vibrating and yielding lips as she returned the delicious favor. He whispered love growls into her ears, endearments mixed fluidly with quietly thunderous desire; desire hardly contained. He pressed against her form and ran his lips over the back of her offered neck to the nape and back, over and over.

He untied those cords at sleeves and undid the sash at her waist. Her entranced stare at him fueled him as hearth flame reflected off of her eye surface. This flickering light also highlighted her glowing skin.

She then released her gown from her bountifully curved body. Juria, such a tall man was he, kneeled before her and suckled desperately at her pendulous, jutting breasts; drawing each light chocolate colored nipple into fuller thickness. His blood gushed into his groin and made ample his instrument. His cock lifted vividly to life and pulsed through his material to her. The underside of his glans imagined her to the utmost.

Claire slightly arched her back, cupped a vast breast and presented it more deeply to him as she also dipped her hand into his trousers and easily found his leaden cock. Her movements threw her red rubbed flaxen locks into the fire's radiance and she appeared even more irresistible to him.

He gently dug his fingertips into her tender ass cheeks. She then clasped hands behind his broad shoulders and secured her lean legs around his hips. Juria raised her up and delicately carried her to their warm and giving bed. Her breathing was hushed but clear to hear. Juria was not capable of nor wished to stop the vastly pleasurable vibrations tearing through his cock as he observed her pliant, soft and beckoning shape horizontal. She and he had woven a mighty arras of love now.

As she watched him slowly strip his clothing off, her breathing became obvious and labored. He posed for her briefly as they both reveled in the beauty of the moment.

He touched his thick pointing cock first. It felt so heavy yet defied gravity by its high erection. A translucent drop was created at his cockhead's opening. It was dewy, thick and glistening. His especial desire revealed itself in this manner.

He wrapped a fist around his long, steely feeling shaft and pumped rhythmically. His cockhead quivered and began to swell into a mushroom cap of heat with the drop remaining poised, and then running slickly to the posterior surface.

Claire's dazed expression was belied by the snaking of her fingertips down to her widespread legs, then to her shining opening. Juria crawled onto the bed and sat hunched over her. She removed her pumping fingers from her fissure and stroked her clitoris instead. His primed cockhead smoothly struck at her drenched vault.

Claire begged him to enter her. All doubt between them was dispelled in this instant. Juria was suffused with uncontrolled yet loving appetite for her. He caressed his wanton cock tip over her mound and then fed his seeming limitless length into her. She moaned and writhed on his shaft as if in agony; agony, though, it was not.

Juria had to alter course to satisfy their needs in other than a traditional manner. He yearned for her to be cognizant of how suffused his mind and body was in tasting her. He must have her with his mouth. So he pulled from her, her eyes widening in surprise, and he lay prone between her, pressed his organ into the bed to use as contact while also spreading her vaginal lips open with his hands. Once he had accomplished this maneuver, he gripped her pink bud tightly with mouth and tongue alone.

He rushed his fingers up to her softly resistant nipples and ministered to them lovingly. Her nipples and clitoris stiffened with these efforts of his. He sucked her jewel deep into his mouth and lashed his tongue side to side, vibrating it steadily. Claire inhaled heavily and rocked into him strongly. He absorbed the glorious, miniscule muscle spasms pouring into him from her. She was enveloped in orgasm. She trusted him in this most vulnerable and giving moment and that rendered him ecstatic.

Claire tugged on his outsize cock. He had not yet experienced release as she just had. He was not able to resist her hands. His was fevered and sank his flesh into that oh so tender hot glove of awaiting tissue. She gasped out, "Put it into me deep and fast, hard my wonderful husband!"

Juria did not comply immediately. He was gentle in spite of lust and love blended. He had to elevate the experience even further. He teased her until it drove him wild as well. Juria gave her his massive rod in gradual doses but was finally ready for culmination.

He was goaded into a more rapid pace. That pace tormented him into greater velocity and force of his thrust into her. His throb was intensive and she moaned strongly as he managed less and less restraint. Juncture of their connection pulsated at last into total release. Claire sobbed in joy as Juria exploded powerfully into her. His ejaculate burst from him in jets hot and thick. He panted through the sensations and cried multiple times, "My love, my love."

Claire's head rested upon Juria's bare chest. His heart beat predictably against Claire's eardrum. It was a reassuring posture for him, obviously for her. They were content with one another. They had enlivened their bond this morning. It was as if the days of fear and anxiety were washed from them; as if it were another life with different players.

"I adore you. I am yours without reserve," Juria uttered.

"I will give myself to no other ever again as you are my husband, my mate. It will be so always."

Sleep befell them and it was sound.

Chapter 47

Time to Die

His infatuation, love conceivably, motivated him profoundly. It was late afternoon and shadows were lengthening into exposed sections of Viktoria's abode. He was reorienting his purpose since his responsibility regarding Claire was lifted by Henry.

The main door and bedroom door that had been destroyed by Danika were being rebuilt. As an artisan, Vincent accomplished replacement of the critical entry and was in the midst of finishing the bedroom entry. It was lengthy, tedious work that kept him occupied as he guarded Viktoria during sunlight hours.

He helped, he protected and he empathized. The mystery was that his caring aspect had been all but nonexistent as a young adult. Someday, he would inquire of Henry as to his reason for rescuing Vincent.

Vincent had assumed much but had never gone directly to the source to ask. The clarity for Vincent was absolute in that he scrupulously understood that Henry had singlehandedly saved him from a cesspool existence.

In Viktoria's absence, while she slumbered oblivious, he ruminated over these sorts of issues. In his human incarnation, he was an intellectual, an intrepid thinker. Philosopher was probably a tad grandiose, he smiled. He craved answers though. Without questions, answers were meaningless. So he developed the former in a perpetual chase of the latter.

One answer that he no longer quested after was his devastating attraction to Viktoria. This incited him to a much greater degree than his fascination with Claire, thank god! He certainly did not choose to create trouble for that brave couple.

Viktoria's lure over him, although a vampire, was that she was beautiful, was bright and positive in spirit when she did not covet blood; she had potencies that dazzled and she had an eroticism that blasted him repeatedly. Ultimately he submitted to her since she cast a hypnotic spell over him that overwhelmingly compelled him. The fully peeled onion was that he fell to the commands of his emotions and impulses with her. There was no rhyme or reason beyond that; it just was.

He stored his finishing tools into a little used corner of the area where Hansel and Gretel dozed those many days ago.

Dusk was rapidly advancing and his change was about upon him. Viktoria's transition out of undead anesthesia began as his onslaught surged. He was ready for the wolf to steal him for a while. And the wolf was prepared to partner the night with his vampire.

He did avoid her as she emerged from her casket each night. She was insistent upon immediate blood as she arose. He was passive and gave to her all leeway as she was swallowed by the murky outdoors. This occasion was not routine apparently. Instead, she flowed to his location. "I had dreams, dynamic dreams, while down of my ballet master.

Blood is secondary, sex and release is primary right now!"

He perceived that her eyes glittered with a lusty sheen. And she was stroking his unsheathed organ already. He was mesmerized as he had been on the trail and each and every time that they coupled. It was a reflex that left him defenseless.

She lightly licked at his inner ear margins, leaving a moist path and dusting of hot breath on his sensitive skin. She was alert to the fact that the wolf was particularly responsive to any attention there. As she gripped his shaft more tightly and pumped it lovingly, she said, "I will feed later. I have to have this, you, without delay. You have to stretch me with your huge member."

He was hapless and captive to her every impulse and instruction.

She inched her body away from him so that she could divest herself of her gown. Paralyzed, Vincent trusted her. He had to as he was on her string regardless.

He discerned that she was under self-control anyhow. And his discernments were almost always accurate besides. It was a dangerous game that they both played presently. What he comprehended was that her needs for him alive were as vigorous and vital as his were for her.

He was succumbing to her influence rapidly. The dance of her fingernails upon her flimsy material entranced him.

She swayed her hips before him. His trance intensified. She lanced through her bodice with sharp nails. This fully exposed her as her enormous breasts tumbled towards him.

She positioned her palms behind her head, shut her eyes, turned that head ninety degrees, tightened her already taut rear and thrust her darkly tipped mounds more so at him. Her skin gleamed, her chest heaved with every inhalation and her juices actually crept down her inner thighs.

"I require you to stay on all fours my gorgeous monster with a monster cock." He was able to tell this comment amused her as she quietly intoned this as if to herself.

He remained exactly as she had requested. Could he have done other?

She bent her knees, balanced herself with sinuously feminine arms and laid herself upon her back. "Advance upon me."

She spread her legs and lips at juncture as Vincent did as ordered. She grasped his shaft again and then filled herself with it. She groaned incessantly. He mounted her from above and hammered into her. His eyes remained open but he visualized nothing.

Elevating feeling gripped him.

She pulled his shaggy head to her. As her excitement gathered, she dragged his upper body downward.

They were on the verge. She seized him closer as they neared climax. His animal load shot into her, she pulsed into an orgasm that surely swamped over and around her and drove all her consciousness from her.

She mechanically scraped her fangs against his neck and then he experienced an overwhelming pain as she drove those fangs into him. He heard as she lapped in abandon at his spurting crimson. His awareness faded. Cruelly, his final thought was, time to die.

Chapter 48

Soft Wisdom

Henry stooped with her in the garden. He tended blooms as energetically as she. Their soiled knees definitely attested to that.

They had bent in prayer in their miniature church already. And these two activities in unison had been at her husband's behest.

So many changes in him she noticed. He was physically present with her in activity after activity.

He suggested a majority of them for their mutual participation each day.

He listened to her intently.

He desisted with his gruff and arrogant mandates to her, to their staff.

He paused more frequently and she often would come upon him as he gazed out beyond his property to environs beyond his own.

"You are fundamentally a good man Henry. I was uncertain those several days ago but took your position nonetheless. I hated myself for it. And in the hating, I despised you as well. I prayed that we might find our route out of what had become an excruciatingly devastating dilemma.

I had a faith that you would rise out of yourself. If you had not, I was planning on tearing that goodness out of you!"

Henry was silent. Then he revealed more of his fundamental self.

"I was disgustingly foolish in my certainty that Danika was to prevail and that the greatest that we would wrest from her was her willingness to permit short visits with Hansel and Gretel. The true shame was that I only considered my wishes, not even yours."

His abashed attitude impressed Adelaide. He was so seriously sincere, she rejoiced internally.

"Imagine yourself as a younger man. You could be surprisingly charitable.

What prompted you to assist Vincent as you did? You essentially remade his life. What was your intent then?"

She observed as he stood up, stretched his spine, wiped his brow with his wrist and returned to the loamy surface but sitting restfully as opposed to genuflecting before the flower buds. He was taking time and consideration before responding to her.

This too pleased her no end. A thoughtful Henry was one of her dearest desires for him.

"It began innocently enough. I had required a distraction from the oft tedious labor involved developing our estate. Vincent was relation who seemed hopelessly mired in a wasting existence. I did not actually believe I could or would be capable of assisting him but felt that his resurrection, were it feasible, was locked in learning of the land underneath his feet.

And who better to teach him about the land than an individual of the land?

As an aside, I believed that at some future point, he might be an asset in acting as my partner.

I was too stubborn then to consider Juria for that. Juria would have been the much better choice had my heart not burned with loathing that he was not of adequate status or quality for our dear Claire. Again, my considerations revolved around me exclusively. As I aided one I unfairly dismissed another."

"Do not dismiss what you gave to Vincent. It was laudable and confirmed for me your essential positive nature.

This image would not leave me as the recent crisis unfolded. It meant everything to hold this image close. Otherwise, you appeared to me selfish, prejudiced and dishonorable as you permitted Danika to pilfer your soul."

"In retrospect, you, my wonderful Adelaide, are absolutely correct.

And thankfully, my unruly emotions spun on me as Juria and I came upon the hideous scene between Danika, Viktoria and Vincent. The children were unbearably compromised. Both Juria and I realized that in the flick of a moment. He was no longer my adversary as he and I picked the children up from the ground and brought them to the safety of the manor house.

Those seconds of coordinated effort wiped my anger from me.

My anger felt appalling. It had jeopardized each and every one of my loved ones. It had sold my own integrity. All of this transformation occurred in a blink. My god that was quite likely the most significant blink of my very full life. I praise creation for it!"

"And I praise creation along with you. Before you and Juria brought the children to the nook safely, I craved my death.

Our daughter had just then spurned and rejected me. The children were being forced to endure the probable demise of their Mother and I had observed my husband and me, out of ire and a complete lack of altruism, defile not only our own covenant but the covenant of our entire family. Meaning escaped me; meaninglessness suffocated me."

Henry moved to her and she comprehended his regard and warmth for her as he wrapped his arms over her shoulders.

They stayed fused for long minutes.

"Yours, my wife, has always been a soft wisdom." Then he guffawed.

"It is a soft wisdom as long as you do not listen to me."

Adelaide hugged him more firmly. "I appreciate the compliment and the jest. Your alteration has cost you much. It took high bravery to release your pride, your control and your dominion over others. Let me inform you that you have triumphed.

I love you beyond my ability to communicate. Thank you so for having rejoined the world and me."

"Will Juria forgive me as you do, Adelaide? Will Claire?"

Forgiveness, once cast, Adelaide now understood, widened larger and larger. Juria and Claire had cast it and her and her husband would be included in its net.

"Yes," she replied.

At that, Henry relaxed without restraint or concern.

Adelaide had not experienced his pure release from the cares and woes of life like this for as long as she could remember. It was, as so much regarding the new Henry, delicious, especial. Could there be truth to the notion that trauma and challenge create opportunities for growth? Adelaide gravely hoped so!

But she instantly asked God if it could be of milder character the next stint. Her old bones echoed this wish.

Chapter 49

So Shocked

She stumbled from her dreams into the waking world. Materializing above her was a pacing Viktoria. Claire bolted upright.

Juria had ducked into the woods before dawn to recoup the hours missed while he and Claire had dallied. So he was not disturbed by Viktoria's presence. The children did not seek Claire out so they must have not heard Viktoria's entry.

Where was her entry? Claire left that cogitation rapidly behind as more insistent issues piled up; in particular the issue of Viktoria's clear consternation and agitation.

"Viktoria, welcome."

"Claire, it is done and I did not intend to do it!"

"What is this about, Viktoria?" Claire was not even entirely awake yet.

"Vincent, it is about Vincent!"

As Claire adjusted to the dark, she shrank back into herself minutely. Faint remnants of blood and gore smeared a fraction of Viktoria's chin. Oh god shrieked Claire's inner faculties.

"I drowned in the ocean of our passions, our intimacies. I had not fed; I reverted and was overwhelmed by my vampire impulses. Oh what have I done? He is mortally wounded and there is no reviving him!"

Claire had not contemplated slapping a vampire, yet she rose on her haunches and did precisely that. She demanded, "His location Viktoria, tell me now!"

Viktoria recoiled and snarled. For that instant Claire was in the utmost of danger but Viktoria held.

"He is in my home. Once I recognized the sickening thing I had done to my love, I thought to rescue him then. I could not. It was useless. Once a vampire, undead law determines that there can be no conversions to anything else. Werewolves are subject to the same rules of post life existence. It was so very sad to watch over him as he passed."

It was an eerie calm that Claire observed from her.

Viktoria stiffened then; she crumpled into her winged mode and she stirred the air massively as she hastily departed the room by penetrating through the glass of the window.

Claire was not about to leave the children or take them in a rush to Viktoria's dwelling. She was not willing to part from them anymore unless they were at school.

She was tempted to walk them to and fro each school day but did not desire to appear overprotective or stunt their social growth in any manner. It was intolerable to conceive of repeating their prior crisis though; to repeat that would be to repeat hell.

So she softly padded to their tiny quarters and cracked the door open smoothly. Hansel and Gretel lay still with chests rising and falling as they should be. All was well in this room.

Claire was so shocked that these grim events had transpired.

Viktoria had shown constructive behavior essentially while they had searched out Hansel and Gretel. Viktoria had retreated from the ménage upon the married couple's request. She and Vincent's mutual adoration had seemed beyond weakening. Vincent and Viktoria had laid Danika to waste as Danika was ready to perform the unthinkable upon her own children. Viktoria had not been compelled to assist her and Juria whatsoever. Yet what did she do? In defense of Hansel and Gretel, she had slain Danika. Without her and Vincent, the children would have been undead forever.

There was her vicious side that all vampires possessed. Yet she shielded Claire and Juria from this. She did not slaughter and feed in their presence. For that Claire was exceedingly thankful.

As to Vincent's raw and wretched passing, well, she had loved him in the too brief days of their tracking and sharing. He had preserved her survival many times over as he minded her safety; she guessed that there were multiple occasions that she was oblivious to.

How grateful she was; to her Father also, in spite of his somewhat twisted rationale, for his having initiated that unknown connection.

Vincent's death left a cavernous thudding in her gut. She would grieve his absence terribly and miss him sorely. Even as a werewolf, he was dear and kind, if that could be imagined. He was unique.

She had perceived Viktoria's sheer desolation just now. She comprehended Viktoria's capabilities both destructive and creative. What else was she, Claire, to do? She pardoned the being her undead reflex.

Claire waited for the children to wake. They would not be privy to this information. They had experienced too much already. They would be protected from this additional tragedy.

She planned on unwinding the entire sorry disaster to Juria upon his appearance home though.

Chapter 50

Rampant Revenge

A tired Juria thumped through the entry, in want of ax sharpening as he had labored so diligently.

He was encased in a thin shell of dried sweat and his work garb required immediate attention. Claire washed those poor battered and patched items with a board and tub at streamside. Special vigor was in order for this round.

For himself, he chose to postpone his dunk in the stream until his weekly schedule of superficial cleansing arrived. Then he would take the bar of soap newly purchased by Claire with him. She insisted and he complied.

This soapy object, this recently available miracle of hygiene, was shared by the four of them and was scrupulously secured by Claire as it was a luxury that they afforded at her command.

Claire greeted him and tugged on his hand and led him to their meal area. She drew out one of their wooden chairs and pushed his shoulders downward. He was compelled to take a seat. Claire fronted him in her chair across the table. She repositioned the vase full of delicious smelling fragile blooms so that she viewed him without hindrance. She reached across the slightly roughened surface and interlaced her fingers with each of his now outstretched arms and hands. She squeezed them definitely, yet lovingly, he sensed.

She was about to deliver something potent his way.

"My sweetest man, Juria; I have difficult news to share with you. Brace yourself please my love.

Vincent has passed!"

Juria was stunned! He sucked his breath in sharply and his chest stung as he did that.

Claire shifted her position and came to him delicately, then laid her cheek to his ear. He extended backward with moisture shining at the outer corners of each eye and whispered to Claire, "How could this be? He is so vital. He is, was, oh god, he was our savior.

Once I laid my initial suspicions aside, just after he provided us food and drink along the trail, I did, I cherished him from then on. Human or wolf, he was righteous. He protected you so consistently.

And then, as he charged Danika, he preserved Viktoria, Hansel and Gretel's lives. Henry and I witnessed that occurrence.

He was valiant and true! How did he die my love? How did such a horrendous event occur?"

Claire laid her lips at the top of Juria's head. He waited patiently. The shock was passing but a tight knot was developing inside him.

Claire heaved her head upwards and backwards, sighed despondently and whistled her exhalation out clearly. He recognized this was excruciating for them both.

"It was as he and Viktoria were in each other's embrace. Viktoria failed to restrain herself, her undead self, and tore his neck apart. She did that involuntarily, the basest of vampire reflex responding.

She appeared here this morning, still dark, to disclose this to me. You had barely left prior to her arrival. She was distraught. Please Juria, do not blame or condemn her!"

His abdominal knot transformed into intense bursting fire evolving into stubborn ember.

Viktoria was the source of this epic slaughter of quality flesh and function.

It was in the midst of this smoldering burn of his that Claire interposed with these words, "She did not hesitate to aid us. She rescued Hansel and Gretel equal to Vincent. She feels his departure as we do."

"Not as we do, my wonderfully giving Claire. She craves to be pure and decent, that I acknowledge. She is, at her core, vampire though. That overwhelms the charity within her. In crisis, she is frightfully dangerous."

"There was no greater crisis than as Danika fled with the children. Viktoria acted bravely and beneficially then. What is your reply to that?"

Juria did respond immediately, "When she must feed, no one is safe or secure!" He articulated this statement firmly, word by slow word.

"I weigh in on the side of her better instincts."

"And I do not."

"Do nothing foolish Juria! I beg of you!"

"I must avenge Vincent's death. I will pursue her and she will atone."

Juria exited the cottage in a fury. He was alert to the fact of Claire's thunderstruck surprise. At this moment, he did not care. He found himself vibrating with a harsh need for rampant revenge against Viktoria.

He ran no more than several strides out of the cottage when he clutched his stomach, bent double and rolled onto the ground. He wept openly.

Claire burst out after him and kneeled to his aid.

He desired hugging her but was certain that he would relent in his determination to track Viktoria and bring justice to the world if he were to warm to Claire's embrace.

He had to resist. If she loved him through and through, she would understand what he was about to do next.

Juria scooted away from Claire.

He uttered, "I love you" and then stood, regained his equilibrium and fled northward without plan.

Chapter 51

Fleet of Foot

Claire had the children in hand and was explaining to them the reason behind their retracing their steps back to her parent's estate as quickly as possible. She begged them to be fleet of foot. Hansel and Gretel were pale and Claire knew that they were in a large degree of shock and discomfort. Claire was equally as flummoxed. She, as the only adult amongst the three, was attempting to keep her wits about her. She would much rather have collapsed, wept or angrily screamed sense into her crazed husband. She must see to the children's welfare first and foremost; not allowing emotions to interfere and derail safety for them all. Were peace and tranquility ever to prevail she wondered?

ABOUT THE AUTHOR

Jeffrey Underwood graduated from the University of Washington with a degree in psychology. Though he has practiced as a Registered Nurse for many years, he comes from a family of published authors. This work of his is his first serious attempt at writing as he has no prior published works. He currently resides in a suburb of Seattle, Washington and hopes that those who sample this tale enjoy the read.